Her whole being was reacting to him. Jasper looked like the man she had felt so close to, the man she had longed to see again, but he struck her as even more guarded than he had been in the first moments when they had met.

"I need to tell you something."

He lifted inquiring brows.

Vienna took a few faltering steps toward him, searching for the man who had shown her those brief moments of tenderness and understanding, but all she saw was enmity.

"This is hard to say." The desire to put this off nearly overwhelmed her, but this was why she was here. To tell him. She needed him to know.

"I'm pregnant," she whispered.

Four Weddings and a Baby

You are cordially invited to...the scandal of the wedding season!

In a shocking turn of events, the marriage of billionaire Hunter Waverly, aka the groom, was halted today when it was revealed he has a secret baby with a local waitress! Their one night clearly wasn't enough...but will this be a real-life Cinderella story?

And the drama doesn't stop there. Our sources say humiliated bride Eden decided to take matters—or should we say, the diamond ring—into her own hands and eloped with best man Remy Sylvain! Well, those two have always had a special connection since that night in Paris...

Meanwhile, maid of honor Quinn is rumored to have been whisked away by Eden's brother, Micah. And the groom's sister, Vienna? Let's just say, she has the biggest secret of all...

It's never a dull moment at a billion-dollar society wedding!

Don't miss Hunter and Amelia's story in
Cinderella's Secret Baby

Read Remy and Eden's story in
Wedding Night with the Wrong Billionaire

Discover Micah and Quinn's story in
A Convenient Ring to Claim Her

And enjoy Vienna and Jasper's story in
A Baby to Make Her His Bride

All available now!

Dani Collins

—

A BABY TO MAKE HER HIS BRIDE

ISBN-13: 978-1-335-58434-2

A Baby to Make Her His Bride

Harlequin Enterprises ULC
22 Adelaide St. West, 41st Floor
Toronto, Ontario M5H 4E3, Canada
www.Harlequin.com

Printed in U.S.A.

Recycling programs
for this product may
not exist in your area.

Canadian **Dani Collins** knew in high school that she wanted to write romance for a living. Twenty-five years later, after marrying her high school sweetheart, having two kids with him, working at several generic office jobs and submitting countless manuscripts, she got The Call. Her first Harlequin novel won the Reviewers' Choice Award for Best First in Series from *RT Book Reviews*. She now works in her own office, writing romance.

Books by Dani Collins

Harlequin Presents

One Snowbound New Year's Night
Innocent in Her Enemy's Bed

Four Weddings and a Baby

Cinderella's Secret Baby
Wedding Night with the Wrong Billionaire
A Convenient Ring to Claim Her

Jet-Set Billionaires

Cinderella for the Miami Playboy

Signed, Sealed...Seduced

Ways to Ruin a Royal Reputation

The Secret Sisters

Married for One Reason Only
Manhattan's Most Scandalous Reunion

Visit the Author Profile page
at Harlequin.com for more titles.

To Doug, who has been my sounding board through this whole series, cheerleading me through the rough patches and celebrating with me when I finished each one. Thank you for your profoundly endless patience. I love you.

CHAPTER ONE

VIENNA WAVERLY PARKED outside the house she owned but had never seen.

Her brother, Hunter, had bought it a month ago, in the most bizarre way.

"Can I use your numbered shell to buy a house without telling you why?" he had asked. "It's nothing criminal, I swear."

"I didn't think it would be, but I thought you were dissolving those." They each had a shell company that Hunter had set up to protect their assets while they'd been in litigation with their stepmother.

"I will, but this came up," he had said.

"What did?" Vienna liked to think she and her brother were close, but it was more accurate to say they were close—adjacent. Kitty-corner. They always had the other's back, but they also kept things from each other, usually in an effort to protect. She loved Hunter to bits and would do anything for him, but this had been a very odd favor.

"It's fifty years old," he had continued in his brisk, close-the-deal manner. "Off-grid, upgraded with solar and water filtration. Great location. The current owners run it as a vacation rental, so it's furnished and in good repair. I'll take it offline, though. There won't be any maintenance or management to worry about. I'll cover all the fees and taxes and explain why I want it in a few months. Then you can do whatever you want with it. Until then, you can't mention this to anyone, not even Neal."

She had barely been talking to her soon-to-be ex-husband, so that had been an easy promise to make.

"Does Amelia know about it?"

"I'll tell her." Hunter had left a distinct pause. "When the time is right."

He had only been married five or six weeks at that point, to a woman who had kept secrets of her own—including the fact that she'd had Hunter's baby. There'd been a massive scandal over the revelation, including his last-minute cancellation of his wedding to one of Vienna's best friends.

Since then, Hunter and Amelia had seemed to be falling for each other. If he was hiding something this big from his new bride, however, that was a huge red flag.

"I need your answer now, Vi," he'd prodded.

"That's really all you're going to tell me?"

"Yes."

Since there were also things she wasn't ready to tell him, she had felt obliged to trust him even though he was leaving her in the dark. "All right. Yes. Go ahead."

"Thank you." He'd sounded relieved. "I wouldn't do it if it wasn't important."

"I know."

She would not have leaned on Hunter's executive assistant to get here without any trace appearing in her own accounts if it hadn't been important, either. She would eventually reimburse all the expenses for her two chartered flights, her company credit card and her temporary phone on the Wave-Com account, but dropping off-grid was exactly what she needed right now.

When she had landed in Nanaimo, on British Columbia's Vancouver Island, a company-leased SUV had awaited her with a full tank of gas and all the groceries she would need. She hadn't told Hunter's PA where she was going, but had asked him to forward her new number to Hunter so he would have it when he needed it.

When the proverbial poop hit the propeller, was what she had meant.

That would happen shortly after Neal was served his divorce papers. Vienna's PR team was cued up with instructions to go on the offensive at that point, with statements that the divorce was a fait accompli.

Never in her life had she been such a sneaky, cutthroat person, but her requests for a quiet, uncontested divorce had been met with faux hurt, promises they could continue trying for a baby, and subtle threats about going to the press with a tell-all about the Waverlys.

That had been last year, when Hunter had been steeped in that ugly court case with Irina, their stepmother. Vienna hadn't wanted to add to his stress with her own drama, so she had simply asked Neal for space. She began spending all her time at their apartment in Toronto while he remained in Calgary, where he was Wave-Com's VP of Sales. She had quietly changed her driver's license, redirected her mail and opened a separate bank account. As long as she maintained the illusion that they were happily married, making herself available for Neal's work engagements and inviting him to a handful of her family appearances, Neal hadn't cared.

She *told* people they were separated, though. Not a lot of people, but solid character witnesses for when the time came.

Nevertheless, she knew Neal would play the victim and say this had come out of the blue. He would claim he wanted to reconcile. There was too much money at stake for him to go quietly. Too much cachet in being Hunter Waverly's brother-in-law.

This story would be yet another gold mine for the clickbait sites, but scandal was unavoidable. That was what Vienna had come to accept. The best she could do was exactly what she'd done. She had waited until Hunter had left with Amelia on a belated honeymoon so the blast radius wouldn't scorch them too badly.

Now she was taking cover herself to ride out the fallout. The address on the conveyancing documents had brought her to Tofino, one of the soggiest places in Canada, located where the western edge of the country dropped into the brine of the Pacific Ocean.

Neal didn't know this house existed. Only her lawyer knew where she had gone.

Soon, she promised herself. Soon she would

be divested of the worst mistake of her life. She would be free to do what *she* wanted.

With a sigh of relief, she stepped from the SUV. After the long drive across the island, her body thanked her for the stretch. Her nostrils drank in the cool fragrance of cedar and pine and fir. The chatter of squirrels hidden in their boughs was cheerfully deafening, drowning out the rush of the ocean against a shoreline she couldn't see.

She left everything in the vehicle, wanting to see inside first. It was supposed to have solar power and a well so she assumed she would have functioning electricity and plumbing, but she had a propane camp stove and a large jerry can of water just in case.

The tall, skinny house had probably been avant-garde in its time, built over the edge of an embankment like this. A narrow wooden walkway, reminiscent of a drawbridge, took her from the graveled driveway to a pair of entry doors flanked by stained glass windows.

She would bet anything that sunshine had not broken through these panels in at least a decade. Nature had closed in around the structure, giving it a distinct "forgotten castle swallowed by brambles" vibe, complete with a moat of empty air between the wraparound veranda and the tree trunks that stood sentry a few feet away.

Maybe a tree house was a better comparison. Either way, she was in love. The siding might be weathered gray, and she imagined the roof was more moss than shingles, but she understood what it was like to be neglected for years, yet still hold potential. This was the perfect place for a dejected princess to shake off the spell she'd been under and awaken into her new life.

The paperwork promised that the keypad on the door had been returned to its factory setting, which was four zeroes, but when she punched that in, it didn't work.

Annoyed, she walked around to where another small bridge connected a side door to the garage. Both of those doors were locked, so she continued to the back.

Here the deck opened into a massive outdoor lounge and dining area with a barbecue built for crowds. The expansive view of the ocean over the treetops stopped her in her tracks.

Wow. Thank you, Hunter.

She took a few deep breaths, grounding herself in the moment so she would remember it, then turned to the two sets of sliding doors interspersed with three wide picture windows.

Clean windows, she noted with a shiver of premonition. It struck her that the deck was swept clean of needles, the furniture was all right side up with the blue-and-yellow-striped cushions in place. The barbecue was uncovered.

Wait a minute. Was that door *open*? The screen was closed, but the glass behind it was wide open.

Her heart tripped as she scraped the screen out of her way and saw that yes, she was able to walk right in.

She expected—hoped?—to see water damage on the floor. That would mean that the previous owners or a property agent had irresponsibly forgotten to lock up properly, but no, it was clean as a whistle in here. Everything was in good order.

With her heart battering her rib cage, she took in that there had been updates carried out over the years. The floors were not the dreaded shag carpet or yellowed linoleum. There was a bright blue-and-black mat that she stepped on as she called out, "Hello?"

She was every idiotic woman who had gone down to the basement in a horror movie, but a more rational side of her mind was telling her some vacation renters had been given faulty information.

Was she even in the right house?

"Hello? Is anyone here?"

The floor plan was an open concept arranged around a massive river stone chimney. On her right, the kitchen had been given a complete makeover with Shaker-style white cupboards and granite countertops. The oval dining table was antique oak, the sitting room furnishings out of fashion but in good repair.

Her gaze lurched back to the wooden bowl on the table. That fruit was real! Two green bananas, an orange and a bright red apple with a sticker on it.

Through the open tread stairs that rose from the back of the sitting room, she could see a desk in the window near the front door. There was a laptop on it, closed, but plugged in with a coffee mug beside it.

Someone was definitely here!

In fact, steps inside the pantry began to creak under the weight of someone climbing them.

Snakes began to writhe in her middle as her morbid gaze stared into the open door of the pantry. This was *her* house, but she wasn't an idiot. She turned to leave the way she'd come in.

"Who are you?" The rumble of a deep, unfriendly voice behind her lifted the hairs on the back of her neck.

She turned back and found not a scruffy squatter, but a fit, well-kept thirtysomething in a gray T-shirt and gym shorts, one who radiated the dangerous energy of a gathering storm.

Her senses were *accosted* by lake-blue eyes that pierced so far into her soul she shivered. His jaw was clean-shaven and looked hard as iron. The glower he wore was even harder. His legs were planted like hundred-year-old oak trees.

He looked her up and down as though she were a squirrel he'd have to shoo out with a broom. His thick brows went up, demanding she answer.

Habits of a lifetime had her wanting to make an apology and slink away. *I'm nobody.* Confrontation had never worked out for her, but she had to start standing up for herself. She wasn't actually in the wrong here, even though he was making her feel that way.

"Who are *you*?" She kept her tone polite, but chilly. "This is my house."

"No, it's not." His confidence was so absolute, it caused uncertainty to roll in her abdomen, instantly putting her on the defensive.

"I can show you the proof on my phone—"

She looked to her hands and found only a key fob. She'd left her phone in the car, but, "This is 1183 Bayview Drive. That was the number on the post at the end of the drive." She pointed in that direction.

His thick brows crashed together.

Ha. She was relieved to have scored a point for once in her life. See? She was not always wrong.

"Kindly explain why you're in my house," she repeated.

His eyes narrowed further. "Vienna?"

Her heart lurched. She'd come here hoping not to be recognized.

Jasper Lindor was about to start his daily workout in the basement when he heard someone try the keypad on the front door. He had changed the code when he arrived here, but a contract killer wasn't likely to try a legal entry anyway. Nor was law enforcement.

He listened to a single pair of light footsteps follow the wraparound deck to check the side door then move to the deck at the back.

Had someone found him or was this person lost? Either way, he was annoyed. He was in the middle of placing a thousand dominoes with delicate precision. He needed another month before he could tip the first one and knock them all down. He didn't want that jeopardized.

When he heard the screen door scrape and the call of a female voice, he let out a hacked-off sigh.

She wasn't trying to hide her presence, so Jasper didn't, either. He came up the stairs to the inside of the pantry only to find her leaving.

She had a spectacular ass. That was his first base impression. Snug jeans cupped a beautiful heart-shaped rump. Her sleeveless top exposed arms that were toned and tanned. Her long hair hung loose to the middle of her back. The brunette color held ash-blond highlights, the sort that pricey salons dispensed. All of her gleamed with the polish only money could buy.

Real estate agent? He should have let her leave, but recent betrayals had made him into the suspicious sort. Had she planted something while she was here?

"Who are you?" he demanded as he swept the rooms with his gaze.

She turned around and— Damn, she was lovely.

His guts twisted as he took in the wavy hair framing wide cheekbones and a flawless complexion. Beneath her peaked brows, her gray-green eyes took him in. Her narrow chin came up.

"Who are *you*?" She gave off an aloof, condescending air, the kind that still had the power to needle him all these years later, when he was no longer the broke teenager standing in a grocery store parking lot. "This is my house."

"No, it's not." He knew who owned this house, but even as she rattled off the house number, his brain made the outlandish connection to the handful of photos he'd seen online.

"Vienna?"

She stiffened. Confusion shifted in her eyes as she tried to place him. Wariness.

"Did Hunter send you?" His thoughts belatedly leaped to his sister and her new baby. "Did something happen?"

"*I'm* asking the questions," she insisted in a haughty way that grated. Her jaw lifted a notch so she was looking down her nose at him. "Who are you? This house is supposed to be empty." She faltered as though mentally reviewing whatever data she'd been given. "At least, Hunter said it wouldn't be used for vacation rentals anymore. Does he know you're here?"

"Yes." Jasper grew cautious himself. He wasn't reassured to learn his intruder was Hunter's sister. She seemed genuinely surprised the house was occupied and didn't seem to know who he was, but she could still ruin his plans.

"Do you work for him? Who are you?" she demanded.

"You really don't know?"

"Would I ask if I did?" Her knuckles were white where she fisted her hands at her sides.

Interesting. She wasn't as full of lofty self-assurance as she was trying to seem.

He gave his clean jaw a rub. Keeping his beard off was a nuisance, but he was relieved to know that it had changed his appearance enough from his own dated online photos that she didn't recognize him.

"Tell me first why you're here. Are you with anyone? Your husband?" She had one, he recalled with a flick of his gaze toward the windows that looked onto the driveway. "Someone else?" he added with a twist of his lips.

A flash of indignation crossed her expression. She didn't like being called unfaithful. Something more vulnerable followed—perhaps a realization that she was alone with a stranger because she lifted her chin and spoke with bold dishonesty.

"My husband is right behind me. You should definitely leave before he gets here."

"Don't lie to me, Vienna," he said wearily. "I hate liars." He really did.

"Well, I dislike people who pretend they know me when they don't. Are you going to tell me who you are and what you're doing in my house?"

"Your house." He ran his tongue over his teeth, still judging that a fib.

She took fresh issue and stood taller.

She was on the tall side for a woman, with a figure that was willowy but indisputably feminine. Pretty. So damned pretty. He couldn't help noticing even though she was very married.

Beauty on the outside didn't mean beauty on the inside, he reminded himself starkly.

But the fact that she hadn't known he was here, and didn't recognize him, told him she wasn't working for REM-Ex.

"I'm Jasper Lindor, Amelia's brother."

She seemed to stop breathing. She stood so still only her lashes quivered as her gaze bounced from his hairline to his gym shoes.

"Do you have proof?" she asked shakily. "Amelia was told you were dead. Hunter wouldn't keep something like this from her."

"She knows I'm alive. So does our father. I've seen them." Once. It had been too short a visit, both heartening and heartbreaking. "I'm not ready to go public on the reasons for my disappearance, so Hunter let me stay here."

She tucked in her chin. Her brow crinkled as she tried to decide whether to believe him.

If trust was a two-way street, they were both circling the block, unwilling to turn onto it.

"My passport is upstairs." Worse for wear after all this time, but he'd managed to hang on to it. "Shall I get it?"

"No. I see the resemblance," she murmured, her gaze traveling over his features with a thoroughness that made his chest itch. She cocked her head, relaxing a little. Her tone warmed. "Is this why Hunter was so strange about buying this property? I had no idea you were alive or staying here. That must have been such a relief for your family to learn you were okay."

"Okay" was a stretch. He barely slept. He was haunted by the death of his friend and couldn't help feeling threatened by a woman who posed as much physical danger as a knitted blanket.

None of that could be erased or fixed, but he was taking steps to achieve some justice. It all hinged on keeping that fact he was alive, and back in Canada, under wraps a little longer.

"Why are you here?" he asked bluntly.

She sobered. A flash of injury in her eyes was quickly screened by her lashes. Her mouth pursed.

"Seeking some 'me' time."

"And you picked this house? Out of all the houses your family owns?" He didn't know exactly how many there were, but he would bet there were several condos, cottages and cabins to choose from.

"I'm allowed to come to a house that *I* own."

From what he'd read—and he'd read very little about her because she hadn't seemed relevant to his situation—Vienna had struck him as the quintessential vapid heiress: feckless and superficial. She was always pictured in the most classically perfect clothing, wearing the same meaningless smile whether attending a fundraiser or an award banquet or her brother's canceled wedding. She didn't have a job, didn't have kids, and somehow kept her head above water despite a habit of flooding proverbial toilets.

"Well, this house is occupied. I want to be alone, too." He tilted a flat smile at her. "That's why no one knows I'm here."

"I wouldn't have come if I'd known," she said in a burst of defensiveness. She folded her arms and glanced over her shoulder to the

SUV in the driveway. "I can't go anywhere else, though. Someone will recognize me. The gulls will flock in."

"Gulls?"

"Paparazzi." She curled her lip in rueful disgust. "I'm embarking on the latest mile of the Waverly Walk of Shame: *divorce*." She lifted her brows facetiously to emphasize what a disgrace that was in some eyes.

All he heard was *paparazzi*, "You're bringing reporters to my doorstep?" His blood pressure shot up to pound behind his eyeballs. *"Come on, lady."*

She jerked her head back, eyes brightening.

"It's not *your* doorstep. It's *mine*," she reminded snippily. "And no, I took precautions. No one knows I'm here. That SUV is leased by Wave-Com. I have a burner phone like some kind of drug lord and my PR team use a secure chatroom. I went to a lot of effort to insulate myself—and Hunter, and Amelia, and Peyton—from what will be a feeding frenzy. I refuse to stand in the pillory anyway, just because my presence here is inconvenient for you. This is my house. I'm staying right here."

Fighting for control over your own life was terrifying. Jasper was a very intimidating man, crossing his arms so those mountains he called shoulders seemed to bunch even higher.

Hunter wouldn't be helping him if he was dangerous, she reassured herself. In fact, Hunter had sworn this house wasn't being used for anything criminal. Jasper wasn't a fugitive evading justice, just a really imposing recluse who was annoyed because his privacy had been invaded.

"We're adults," she pointed out, trying for a more conciliatory tone, but she could feel the strain in her voice. "Family."

She offered a welcoming smile, genuinely happy to meet Amelia's brother, but for some reason their gazes clashed like steel on steel, sparking and hot. Her throat felt scorched.

His glower rejected her overture and his disapproval rolled toward her like a fugue, seeping into the heart of her insecurities.

Not you. You're not wanted. Get lost.

She resisted giving in, refusing to run like a coward. It was *her* house.

She waved at the wide rooms around them.

"I'm sure we can make this work. We both seem to be motivated to keep our presence here quiet." She certainly was. "It seems like a big enough place that we should be able to share it without getting in each other's way. I brought my own groceries."

One dark brow lifted, unimpressed.

"I'm only staying a week." Once the initial shock wave passed, she would fly to Europe to attend a wedding. "I have to be seen in public at least once before Hunter and Amelia get back. I'll surface in Toronto so they won't be inundated at their home in Vancouver." Hopefully. "I have a *plan*. This isn't my first time in the goat rodeo of bad publicity."

He snorted.

"I won't even make noise! I brought my art things." So she could finally work on her own projects, rather than curating finished pieces for others. "Are you really going to refuse to let me stay here?"

"I can't, can I?" His voice dripped sarcasm. *"Mi casa es tu casa."*

CHAPTER TWO

WHAT A GRUMP.

Vienna walked outside to collect her bag and exhaled a huge sigh of bottled-up tension. Was she out of her mind to stay? His attitude was pretty much her worst nightmare, having grown up with her stepmother radiating that same pained tolerance.

It's my house, she reminded herself.

But she really should start communicating more frankly with her brother. He'd been going through a lot with his new marriage and new baby, so she hadn't wanted to be a bother. She *never* wanted to be a bother, but nearly everyone treated her as though she was.

She needed to grow up and grow a pair. She knew that. She needed to stop worrying about what other people thought of her and go after what she wanted without shame or guilt.

She had come this far on that journey already, hadn't she? This was not the time to let her courage fail her.

Yet, when she walked back in to face Jasper's judgmental gaze, and the sensation that he saw all her flaws clear as day, it took everything in her to say, "I'll take one of the guest rooms. Don't worry about moving out of the big one."

His snort as she sailed under his nose suggested he was not worried at all, but she held her head high as she took her suitcase up the stairs.

She set it down in a bedroom that was adjoined to another through a Jack and Jill bathroom. A brief exploration showed her a reading nook on the landing then she peeked into the primary suite where the blue-and-yellow decor was fresh and bright. The room was dominated by a pillow-topped king-size mattress in what looked to be a waterbed frame built of massive timbers. Light poured in through the glass doors to a balcony with a limitless view of the ocean.

Aside from a bookmarked spy thriller on the night table and a flannel shirt hanging over the back of a chair, the room looked unoccupied.

Amelia had always made Jasper sound so human. Her stories were always mixed with distress that he was missing, but now Vienna thought about it, Amelia's mood had lightened recently. Vienna had thought it was more to do with how well she and Hunter had been getting along, and the honeymoon to the South Pacific that they had impulsively planned, but now she thought perhaps the switch had happened when Amelia had learned her brother was alive.

For Amelia's sake, Vienna was thrilled that Jasper had survived his disappearance, but he certainly wasn't anything like the doting brother Amelia had described. He seemed embittered and gruff. Hard.

Maybe that's just how he feels about you.

Stop it. She had been to therapy. She knew self-defeating thinking when it rang in her head.

Actually, that ringing was the door chime. He was going in and out while she was lingering up here, avoiding him.

She made herself go back downstairs and found Jasper had brought in most of her groceries.

"*How* long are you staying?" he asked, and set down the insulated box holding meat and dairy.

"I like to cook and knew I'd have time."

The reality of sharing a house with him caused her stomach to pitch. She had never been so aware of a man. Not in this way. She'd suffered the friction of a difficult marriage where more went unsaid than was ever acknowledged aloud. Simply being a woman meant she'd endured the company of men who made a woman feel unsafe, but that wasn't why she felt so uncomfortable right now.

Physically, she sensed no danger from Jasper. Emotionally? His unfriendliness stepped right on her old bruises. She was right back to feeling that every word or deed could be a giant misstep while she felt obliged to get along because their siblings were married.

Don't make waves, Vienna.

It had always been her job to make everyone else feel comfortable, no matter what it cost her. She fell back on that habit as he came back with the jerrican of water.

"I was planning to make halibut tonight. There's enough for two."

He put the jerrican down in a corner on the floor. His casual strength was mesmerizing, but the way he eyed her as if looking for a catch kept a wall of antagonism between them.

"I thought we were going to stay out of each other's way." He picked up the little sack of fair-trade coffee beans and tucked it into a cupboard.

"We're—" She didn't dare call them family again. "In-laws. We should get to know each other." Maybe then she would quit feeling like she was walking on hot coals.

"I know who you are, Vienna," he said pithily.

"Really? How?" She prickled under his laser-sharp stare, feeling painfully transparent yet affronted. How could he possibly know anything about her when she had no inkling herself? She had lost any sense of self years ago. "Online trolls, I suppose?" She was instantly stinging with the poison of false reports. "I'll disregard what your sister has said about you, then, and believe everything *I've* read."

She hadn't read much. Amelia had insisted he wasn't the kind of person to walk away from a job or get someone killed, but that was what he'd been accused of. And maybe Vienna ought to give more credence to that, because the warning that flashed in his gaze was downright lethal.

All he said, however, was, "Touché."

His acceptance of her remark did nothing to alleviate the uncomfortable tension in her belly. She didn't care whether he approved of her. She didn't.

She shouldn't.

She went back to stowing items in the refrigerator.

"I thought this said 'pastille' and you'd brought a huge box of candy." He was holding her brand-new case of *plein air* colors. "You're a pastel artist?"

When she overcame her imposter syndrome enough to call herself any kind of artist, yes, but her whole body wanted to fold in on itself that he was touching her things. It was as if he was looking straight into her and it *hurt*.

"Sculpture," she joked past the suffocating sensations. She crossed to take the box from his hands and tuck it away with her pads and colored pencils, moving the whole lots to the far end of the dining room table. "The hammer and chisel won't bother you, will it?"

"Not while my heavy metal is playing."

He cocked a brow that said, *I can play that game too.*

"I'll pull your car in." He picked up her key fob and exited out the side door, the one that led to the garage.

She let out another pent-up breath and was finishing the groceries when he returned.

"Is there a path to the beach?" she asked. "I'd like to walk off my travel."

And get away from these oppressive undercurrents.

"I'll take you. It's overgrown. You might get lost."

Terrific.

It was August, so the ground was dry and the air warm, but there was coolness in the shadows beneath the boughs of the trees that spoke of old growth and time measured in centuries.

Jasper walked this path every day. It was easy enough to follow, but it would be just like a city girl to wander into the ferns and get disoriented. The last thing he needed right now was to have his *sister-in-law* lost in the woods.

Why did that word bother him so much? They were related by marriage. That was a true fact and, someday soon, he would regain his old life. He would visit his sister and her baby and would cross paths with Vienna and her husband—

No. She was divorcing. That was why she was here. She was taking cover while it was announced. The gossip sites did love a celebrity breakup, but she wasn't a celebrity in the league of an American pop star. How bad could it be? From what he'd read…

Huh. She'd put him in his place on that one,

hadn't she? He'd been subjected to false reports himself, so he had some sympathy on that front.

"What did she say?" he asked over his shoulder.

"Who?" Her voice was farther behind him than he'd realized.

He had spent half his life off-grid, so ducking branches or stepping over roots was as easy as a flat sidewalk for him. He stopped and watched her pick her way carefully down a short drop, clinging to a sapling. She paused to drink in the moss-laden branches around them, expression serene and all the more appealing for that softness.

"My sister," he clarified, yanking his thoughts from where they shouldn't go. "You said you would disregard what she had said about me and believe what you'd read online."

"Oh. Um. I don't know. That everything online was wrong," she said wryly. "That you looked after her when your mom passed and taught her to drive. Things like that. She said you probably would have killed Hunter with your bare hands if you'd been around when she turned up pregnant." She chuckled dryly, but he thought he caught a glimpse of agony in her expression before she blinked and looked curiously to where a crow was cawing in the trees.

"It sounds as though our father was prepared to do that when he showed up at Hunter's wedding." The fact Jasper hadn't been there for Amelia, and had instead caused her and their father untold distress, was a continuous knife of guilt in his belly.

"Tobias was pretty livid," she agreed, smile oddly wistful. "I think it's nice that you're so close, though. It makes me envious."

"You and Hunter aren't close?"

"Not in the same way. Our upbringing was very different from yours."

"Wow." He would go ahead and believe his first impression of her, if that was how she talked. If the opinion of people like her mattered to him, he would point out that his net worth was in the same neighborhood as hers.

"Not because of means," she said, cross and defensive. "Our father remarried. Hunter was tapped to take over the family business and it's not exactly a dry cleaning outlet. He was busy with that so we had a very different upbringing from *each other.*"

"You don't work for Wave-Com?" It was a national communications conglomerate. There had to be room for her.

"No. My—Neal does. He's the VP of Sales and Marketing."

Her ex, he presumed.

"I couldn't believe who Amelia married," he admitted and started walking again, still astonished his sister was married at all.

He'd been in a remote village on a tributary of the Bío-Bío River, tanned deeply enough to pass for a local when a stranger had come looking for the Canadian who was reputed to be staying in the area.

I'm working for your sister's husband. You can trust me, he had said to Jasper in Spanish.

Like hell. Jasper had impatiently waved him away, sending him downstream.

The next day, the man had come back with a story from Amelia's childhood that Jasper genuinely believed she wouldn't share with anyone except someone she trusted. By then, he'd been gone more than a year. A year in which he'd made very little headway, despite constant efforts to raise investigations in Chile. Along with causing a painful loss, REM-Ex had cut him off from more than his family and his resources. He had lost his reputation and very identity.

It had been a gamble to trust that stranger, but he had reasoned that his dad and sister already believed he was dead. He had climbed aboard the private jet and read up on his sister's husband while flying back to Toronto.

"Hunter was about to marry someone else," he recalled. "That doesn't exactly sound like a love match for Amelia." That was eating at him, even though Amelia had seemed happy when he'd seen her.

"Hunter wouldn't have let it get that far if he'd known about Peyton," Vienna insisted behind him. "Eden has since married someone else, too. It all worked out for the best."

"It certainly worked out for me," he said ironically. "I got a free flight back to Canada, but I can't help worrying she married him for my sake."

Jasper pulled his own weight. He solved his own problems. People came to *him* for solutions. He didn't rely on others. It galled him that his sister had had to come to his rescue and he couldn't help wondering what it might have cost her.

"They married for Peyton's sake," Vienna assured him. "It was bumpy at first, but I've never seen Hunter as relaxed as he is around Amelia and Peyton. I don't know what kind of father I thought he would be. Ours was…"

He stopped again, turning to see her cheeks were hollow, her mouth pensive.

"What?" he prompted.

She shrugged it off. "Hunter has always been very supportive and concerned about my welfare, but he's different with them. He's very open and loving, more so than I've ever seen him. It's cute." Her expression softened, then brightened. "Oh!"

She brushed past him to where the trees opened onto the beach.

"I was starting to think the climb back up wouldn't be worth wherever it was you were taking me, but this is beautiful!"

She shaded her eyes as she scanned the cove formed by an arm of treed land extending outward to the south. Ahead, a small island with exactly three trees stood in the water. It was just far enough away that it remained unreachable on foot even when the tide was out. The sky was an intense blue, the sun glittering off the green water, illuminating the foam of the incoming waves. The sand was granite-gray and littered with kelp, utterly empty of human occupation.

The wind dragged at her hair and pressed her clothes to her front. He would have pegged her for a white sand, all-inclusive beach type, not so much raw nature, but she was entranced.

A sense of accord settled over him. He was

a loner and had become very proprietary about this small stretch of paradise, but if he had to share it, he was glad it was with someone who appreciated it.

She glanced at him and caught him staring at her. Her carefree joy faltered into uncertainty.

He looked away, rebuking himself. *Not her.* For many reasons.

"There's a hotel around that outcrop. I walk this direction." He began negotiating the thick fence of gnarled driftwood thrown up on the beach by eons of wind and waves.

Tension filled the silence between them as they walked across the untouched sand.

Vienna told herself it was the breeze playing in her hair, snapping it against her face, that made her feel so sensitized. She was an artist, naturally affected by tangy, earthy aromas. That was why she wanted to take off her shoes, so she could feel the shifting temperatures in the sand. That was why her eye wanted to watch the sunshine paint itself over the planes of his body and the angles of his face.

It had nothing to do with that moment when they had come onto the beach, when she had suddenly felt noticed. *Seen.*

Most people only saw a curated version of

her. She engineered it that way. She hid behind layers of perfect manners and pretty clothes, flawless makeup and carefully styled hair, protecting her thoughts and feelings with whatever image she thought they wanted to see. She was the Wave-Com Heiress or Neal Briggs's Wife. Hunter Waverly's sister or Peyton's Auntie Vienna. She hated that she had to put up all these fronts. It was exhausting, but the nakedness of being herself was worse.

The wildness of the empty beach had called her out of her shell, though. For those vibrating seconds, she'd simply existed as part of the world. She was alive and unstoppable and beautiful *because* of the marks that flotsam and time had left upon her.

Then she realized Jasper had been studying her in her unguarded moment.

How would he use it against her? How would he hurt and diminish her?

"I'll save that for another day," she said when they reached a creek that cut a wide swath across the sand. They couldn't cross it without getting soaked to their knees, so they started back.

She surreptitiously looked at him as he walked in long, powerful strides beside her. His gaze moved constantly, ignoring the beauty of a champagne-like splash of a wave on a rock, or the majestic soaring of an eagle on an updraft. His watchfulness was unsettling, his rigidity adding to her tension.

"How long have you been here?"

"A month."

Before that, he'd been missing for a year. If Amelia hadn't learned she was pregnant, she would have gone to Chile to find him. She had rightfully smelled something fishy in the fact that Jasper's employers had claimed he was dead, but refused to pay out his life insurance.

"You're protecting your family by staying under the radar," she realized.

His gaze raked her. "That's one reason, yes."

"Am *I* in danger?" She touched her chest.

"Not if no one knows we're here," he drawled.

"Only my lawyer, I swear." She held up her hand as if taking an oath. "Hunter doesn't even know what I'm doing, obviously. Otherwise, he would have told me this was not the place to ride things out."

"He doesn't know you're getting a divorce? Why not?"

She'd been afraid he would talk her out of it.

"Call me old-fashioned, but I thought my husband should be the first to know," she said ironically. "Once he receives the papers, I'll tell Hunter."

"Your *husband* doesn't know?" Jasper choked on a humorless laugh. "That's cold."

She lurched to a halt.

"You know *nothing* about my life." *She* was the cold one? Right now, sure, her voice was as frigid as the tundra during an ice age. Her heart had plunged to the bottom of a canister of liquid nitrogen, but Neal was the one incapable of basic human warmth. That was why she was walking away from her marriage and the bleak future he offered her.

Jasper stopped two paces ahead of her.

She willed her hot eyes not to well with tears of rage or, worse, the humiliation that had been such a constant companion all these years. But the deep, horrible suspicion that maybe she was to blame for the lack of love from her husband was always there, ready to choke her.

"You're right." Jasper's cheek ticked. "I was out of line. Your reasons for divorce and how you go about it are none of my business."

Her jaw almost fell to the sand. She really was going to cry now, because at no point in her marriage had her husband ever offered anything close to that sort of personal accountabil-

ity. It was always, *Don't be ridiculous, Vienna.
What about* my *feelings?*

Fearful she would break down completely,
she ducked her head and walked past Jasper
without another word.

Ah, hell. He'd handled that poorly, hadn't he?

Women were more vulnerable than men.
They were vulnerable *to* men. He knew that.
Even the trophy wives he wanted to lump her
in with, the ones who seemed happy to use
their looks to feather their nests, were physically smaller than men. They were objectified
and subjected to sexism.

For all he knew, Vienna's marriage had been
abusive. He had no right to pass judgment on
how or why she had chosen to leave it.

He was trying to hold Vienna at a distance,
though. Trying to dismiss her as avaricious and
manipulative so he wouldn't admire things like
how she moved with the grace of a gymnast.

They had reached the obstacle course of
driftwood between the beach and the forest.
She stepped atop a log and balanced her way
along, shifting to the next and the next as she
worked her way up the beach. She didn't look
back once, which told him how much he had
annoyed her.

He followed, brooding, watching for the path back to the house in case she missed it.

They were almost there when she gave a sideways leap to a log that had been sanded by wind and waves to a smooth, slippery finish. Her foot shot out from under her and she waved her arms, about to topple onto a pile of broken driftwood.

Jasper reacted without thought, leaping to catch her into the front of his body, giving her that extra moment to find her balance again.

It was seconds—less than five—that he held her, but the feel of her slender back and the firmness of that gorgeous ass pressing into his groin left him branded by her shape.

At best, he expected a grudging thank-you, but when he released her and she looked back at him, her expression was startled and defenseless. Her gaze traveled over him as though she was seeing him for the first time. As though she was seeing through his clothes and touching his skin. Or wanted to.

There was such earthy, sexual awareness in her eyes, such wonder when she lifted her gaze to meet his, that it struck him as a delicious punch in the stomach.

He was experienced enough to know when a woman had decided he struck her fancy. He was man enough to consider it when one did. Everything about her appealed to him. Her flowing hair glinted with sunlight. Her soft mouth and naked lips were shiny and receptive. Kissable.

Damn, but he wanted to taste that mouth. Her curves enticed his palms to gather and stroke and something intangible within her called him to a brighter place, drawing him like a flame in the night. Beckoning.

It's not infidelity if she's divorced, the devil on his shoulder pointed out.

It could happen. *They* could.

Theoretically, he corrected dryly, as she blushed with mortification and jumped to the sand, hurrying up the path to the house.

That was probably for the best. An affair with her was a terrible idea.

CHAPTER THREE

VIENNA HAD ALWAYS found an escape in art. Her only true memory of her mother's life was the funeral when she'd been laid to rest. Not even the service, but the aftermath, when a well-meaning aunt had handed her a coloring book and some crayons.

While family and guests had condoled in drab colors, speaking in heavy, somber tones around her, she had scribbled sunset orange and aquamarine against patches of vibrant violet and dusty denim. Hunter had patiently read the labels to her until she knew their names by sight, not yet able to read them herself.

She still reached for colors and patterns when she was agitated—electric lemon and fern green, smooth lines and pleasing balance. It was more than an effort to create order when her life was out of control. It was about taking something difficult and messy and finding the good in it. The beauty.

Given what she'd been through in her lifetime, she ought to be a heralded artist with several showings under her belt by now. Sadly, she had not dropped everything and picked up her sketch pad every time she was overlooked by her father or humiliated by her stepmother or disappointed by her husband. More often than not, she had channeled her emotional energy into creating a better Vienna. Her insecure self had always reasoned that she was the thing that needed work, otherwise all of those people would have treated her better.

Thus, she had learned to use a makeup palette so she appeared prettier. She had learned to accessorize a couture dress with the right designer handbag and custom jewelry. She could arrange flowers and host the perfect party and recover from whatever farce her stepmother turned an occasion into. She had learned to decorate a home so people would think her life within it was magazine perfect even when it was the farthest thing from it.

She didn't know how to gloss over what had happened on the beach, though.

Her foot had slipped. She hadn't been paying attention because she'd already been discon-

certed by that man in a hundred different ways
and when he'd caught her close, something had
happened to her. Her skin had come alive. She'd
felt so sensitized that she'd practically felt the
whorls in his fingerprints against the bare skin
of her arm. A sweeping sensation had flown
through her, like a breeze that picked up all the
brittle leaves within her, wafting them away.

The libido that had never been very strong,
and which had sunk into a veritable coma
through her marriage, had awakened in a blunt
rush. Her lungs had gulped for air as if she'd
been underwater for too long. Polarities in her
blood had aligned to point at him.

He had released her, but slowly, ensuring she
had her balance.

She hadn't.

Her whole world had tilted on its axis.

It had hit her that not being married meant
the wide chest of a man wasn't something to
admire objectively as an artist. It was something that could be attractive in a more physical sense. A carnal sense.

She didn't have carnal feelings, but he was
so close, and the memory of that strong wall
imprinted on her so tangibly, the memory of
wanting to splay her hands across his pecs and
feel him. Explore.

This welling of sensuality was so new, it had felt like a spell. As she looked up at him for an explanation, she'd been mesmerized by the glints of molten silver in his blue eyes.

Her heart had flipped over. The charged air between them shimmered, making colors more vivid, the sound of the waves more lush. When his gaze dropped to her mouth, he'd left a sensation there sharp as a bee sting.

This is desire, she had realized through her haze.

Ironically, she recognized it because she'd never felt anything like it before. She had always been convinced that movies and books exaggerated the basic physiology of arousal, but this flood of heat and awareness was exactly as had been described. A fire had been lit within her, one that softened her knees and made her throat feel tight and held her trapped firmly in the moment.

She wanted things in those charged seconds. Explicit things. His mouth. His touch. The right to touch him back and the knowledge of how his voice sounded when he was aroused. She wanted to know how he smelled and how his body would feel against hers. She wanted his weight upon her and the sensation of him thrusting inside her.

The corner of his mouth had curled with anticipation, sending a fresh spear of white heat into the pit of her stomach.

Panic had then clogged her throat. *He knows, he knows!*

She had turned away, hurrying back here to the house, but there was no escape. She could try to get lost in Caribbean blue and prairie yellow and arctic white, but he would catch up to her eventually.

She sat on the deck off the kitchen, barricaded behind one of her new sketch pads and a fresh box of colored pencils. When she heard him come in through the door to the basement she wanted to die. Crushes were for thirteen-year-olds, not a woman finally taking the wheel of her own life.

He didn't come upstairs right away, though, and she recollected the weights she'd seen in the basement. She had a feeling she had interrupted his workout when she arrived so, when she realized he was staying down there, she relaxed and became more intentional in what she was doing.

Her goal this trip was to work on a portrait of Peyton for Hunter and Amelia. For now, she got to know her colors and paper by calling up different photos of objects that she'd loaded onto a digital picture frame specifically for this purpose.

She was soon immersed in layers of color, playing with pressure and line thickness, only to be yanked from her concentration when she heard the shower come on upstairs.

He was naked up there?

Don't think about it.

She did, though. She clenched her eyes shut, trying not to, but her artist's imagination conjured a vivid image of suds tracking through Jasper's chest hair, down his abdomen and into the crease between his thigh and—

Nope.

But now she was back to dwelling on how obvious she'd been on the beach. She wanted to duck her head into her arms and sob with embarrassment. It had been bad enough when he had acknowledged that he was judging her unfairly. That had pulled the rug out from under her, but then she'd let him see how astonished she was by her own ability to *feel*. How gauche!

The worst part was, now that those stupid feelings had been awakened, they sat under her skin like fresh tattoos, hot and livid and undeniable. She would never be able to hide them again.

The shower cut off.

She frantically swiped through her photos, trying to find something to distract her. There. Her neighbor's cocker spaniel. She forced herself to concentrate on rendering the rippled hair of his square ears and his adorable head tilt of curiosity.

It was so challenging to set those small curved strokes of caramel fur that she lost track of where she was. When the door into the house rolled open beside her, she was startled into gasping and sitting up straight, disoriented by her surroundings.

"I'm starting dinner," he said. "Would you like a glass of wine?"

"You're cooking?" His words didn't make sense. Neither did his impassive expression. Wasn't he going to laugh at her with his eyes and make her feel small for overreacting?

"Unless you prefer raw fish, but I'm no sushi chef. I wouldn't risk it if I were you." The corner of his mouth tilted with self-deprecation.

"No…um. Thank you. Yes, please, to the wine."

She was so taken aback that she had barely gathered her thoughts, let alone her supplies, before he returned with straw-colored wine in a stemless glass. He set it on the table within her reach and turned away to start the barbecue.

"Would you like help?" she offered.

"No. You're busy."

She glanced at her sketch, catching herself before she dismissed it as unimportant. If it was important to *her*, then it was important. Or so her therapist had stressed.

Her page and pencils held little interest for her when she could watch him move with economical efficiency, though.

"What do you do while you're here?" she asked when he came back out to set the fish on the grill. "I don't mean that as a criticism," she hurried to add. "I saw your laptop, so I assume some kind of remote work?"

"That depends on how you define work." He closed the lid on the barbecue and twisted off the cap of the bottle of beer he'd brought outside for himself. "Some of it is research and reports that will serve me once I've cleared my name and can resume my life. I've been compiling evidence and putting other things in place toward that goal. Mostly I'm waiting for a certain someone to come home from international waters, so he can be arrested and held accountable."

"Who?"

"Orlin Caulfield. President of REM-Ex. If he

catches wind that I'm out of Chile and coming after him, he'll stay where he can't be touched."

"What did he do?" She hadn't liked asking Amelia too many questions about Jasper since it had always been such a painful topic for her.

He took a pull off his beer and stared into the trees, his profile like granite. The silence went on so long she decided he wasn't going to answer and looked down to her work again.

"He started by hiring me under false pretenses. Then he got my interpreter killed and has been trying to hold me responsible for it." His features flexed with anguish.

"In Chile? I'm so sorry. Was—" He? She? Did it matter if his interpreter was a man or a woman? A lover or a friend? It was obviously very painful for him. "That's tragic."

"It is." The lines of grief in his face made her hurt for him. Did he blame himself, even though he wasn't responsible? "Saqui was helping me work with the Mapuche. That's how I learned how much environmental damage was already being done by REM-Ex. I had been hired to ride point on a new project, but I raised concerns over what I'd heard and went to see the valley for myself. That's why they claim I walked away from my job site, but I was trying to help the company get ahead of a crisis. I was writing a plan for cleaning up their mess, but their response was 'What mess?'"

"The corruption was coming from inside the house?"

"Exactly. The landslide that killed Saqui was deliberate. Someone set off a charge. I want to believe they were only trying to hide their crime, not commit murder, but either way Saqui was killed." He ran his hand down his face, clearly still tortured by it.

She wanted to get up and walk over to hug him; she felt his pain so deeply, but there was an invisible wall around him, firmly holding her off.

"I was supposed to be there with him." The lines in his face flexed with fresh anguish. "I'd gone into town to email photographs and a report on what I'd seen. Saqui wanted to stay and make more notes. The site was miles away from town, but I know what it sounds like when dynamite drops half a mountain. Emergency crews went out, but they blocked the road and wouldn't let me see it for myself. I went to Saqui's family, hoping he'd turn up there."

He hadn't, obviously. Vienna felt so sick for him. So very sorry.

"REM-Ex called to tell them Saqui had been caught in the rubble and said I was responsible. They said if I wasn't buried with him, I would be arrested for negligence and manslaughter. They didn't realize I was sitting in their kitchen."

"You didn't set off the charge!" she cried.

"No. And I don't run away from my problems," he asserted tightly. "But if that's how they were playing, I couldn't risk arrest. How the hell could I clear my name from a jail cell?"

"So you pretended you had died, too?"

"Not by choice. The first few days I was in the bush, avoiding arrest, but I gave everything I had to Saqui's sister. She took it to the papers, but REM-Ex quashed it, saying it was a hoax. They said I couldn't have written it because I was dead. That was a genius move because it allowed them to cancel my documents and flag my passport if I tried to cross a border or fly. I hated that Dad and Amelia believed I was dead, but given REM-Ex had already killed Saqui, I thought it was safer for them. I didn't think this would drag on for a *year*."

Vienna had been denigrated in many ways, but never accused of a crime. She couldn't imagine how he'd felt at that level of persecution.

"What did you do? Where did you go?"

"Saqui's family want justice for his death as

much as I do. I stayed with some of his relatives, helping on their farm while we tried to get the police to investigate, but REM-Ex has deep pockets. They papered the country in a smear campaign, even pinning their environmental crimes on me, things that happened before I had ever set foot in that country! Thanks to being dead, I was locked out of my accounts and I was afraid to use them anyway. What if someone traced me? I didn't want to put Saqui's family at risk. Or Dad and Amelia. I couldn't afford to underestimate what REM-Ex would do because, even if Saqui's death was an accident, they obviously don't want it coming to light that they caused it. I make a far tidier scapegoat."

"But now you can finally get Orlin What's-his-name arrested? How?"

"The rest of my plans are classified," he said grimly. "No offense, Vienna, but I don't want you screwing up my one chance to catch the bastard who's trying to frame me."

"None taken," she lied, and dropped her gaze to Bowser's red collar.

Jasper woke at 2 a.m. Hard.

It was basic biology that celibacy and a nearby woman would put him in this state, so he ignored it. It wasn't as if she'd done anything to encourage it. Over dinner, they'd talked about incidentals—the climate in Chile and the latest season of a series they had both binged.

He'd been trying to mentally step back after talking about Saqui. Vienna's earnest sympathy had unsealed the door on his anger and grief and he couldn't help feeling she had slipped through in the same breach. It was disturbing enough he'd sought distance after dinner, plugging in his earbuds and checking on his ghost purchases of REM-Ex shares.

Perhaps she'd felt the same need to shore up because she'd gone upstairs and only come down once for a cup of tea before bed.

Not seeing her hadn't meant he wasn't aware of her. She had stayed in his thoughts when he went to bed. It should have been a welcome change from replaying old conversations with Saqui, trying to rewrite history, but he'd only tossed and turned with restless arousal.

When he did drift off, she was right there in his dreams, stepping into his arms instead of running away.

What was it about this woman? He went long stretches without female company. Hell, he had lived alone—often in the wilderness— for weeks at a time. He preferred it that way.

Coming from a close-knit family didn't mean he was a pack animal. At heart, he was a lone wolf.

Which wasn't to say he didn't have relationships. They just died on the vine because of the work he'd chosen. Most people who married did so because they wanted to spend time with that person, not live alone, waiting for them to come home.

Besides, he wasn't ready to let anyone in. Saqui had been the first close friendship he'd had in a long time and Jasper hadn't really had a choice. It had been Saqui's nature to draw people out and make jokes and bring them home to eat with his family.

He'd been young and ambitious and eager to learn everything Jasper could teach him. Jasper had seen himself in Saqui and couldn't stop hating himself for hiring him, inadvertently pulling him into something that had wound up costing him his life. The guilt at not seeing the danger, and not insisting Saqui come to town with him that last, dark day, was unrelenting.

But of all the unique minerals he'd picked up over the years, none had been a crystal ball.

Logically, he knew he hadn't caused Saqui's death, but his self-blame had gone off the scale as REM-Ex had tied his hands against revealing what had really happened. Saqui's family hadn't had any resources to seek justice on their own. They were humble farmers who'd been kept afloat with Saqui's financial help. The best that Jasper could do for them was help them navigate getting a life insurance payment— which had taken forever because it had been bought through Jasper's company and he was "dead."

The Melillas hadn't wanted money anyway. They wanted their son back. Seeing how devastated they were, and how much they missed him, ate holes in Jasper's soul.

This was the real reason he pursued a solitary life. Grief was horrific. Better to hold himself back from risking such crippling pain.

A creak in a floorboard had him lifting his head to see a faint bar of light appear beneath his door. Was that a quiet knock?

He threw back the covers and pulled his shorts over his briefs.

When he opened the door, the hallway was empty. He glanced to where the lamp glowed in the reading nook.

Vienna looked up from where she knelt before the low bookshelf. She stilled and so did he. Neither of them seemed to breathe.

The yellow light and her buttercup nightgown wrapped her in gold. He dragged his gaze from the lace that plunged between her breasts and the gathered silk that cradled the swells so lovingly.

"What are you doing?" He had to clear a thickness from his throat.

"I couldn't sleep and saw these earlier." She held up one of the historical romances.

Goodness, what could be the cause of both of them suffering sleeplessness, he wondered facetiously, even as he imagined dropping one of those strings off her shoulder and pressing his mouth to her luminous skin.

"I knew I wasn't going to turn on my phone while I was away, but I forgot to bring any books." She absently tucked her hair behind her ear as she dipped her head to read the back.

Let me, he thought, imagining the feel of that stud in her lobe against his tongue.

"The vampire one is decent." He leaned his shoulder against the wall. "The duke is dry. The pirate is filthy." In a good way.

"Oh?" The way she brightened with interest and promptly shoved the duke back on the shelf in favor of the sea blue cover of the erotic swashbuckler was adorable. "I didn't expect you would read romance."

"I don't sleep well. I've read everything in this house, trying to nod off. There's a board book in the basement about a hungry caterpillar that almost worked, but the ending got too exciting."

She chuckled and rose. "I'm pretty sure I read that one back when I was learning to read."

Her nightgown only went to the tops of her thighs. He bit back a groan.

"I'm sorry about the insomnia." Her concerned gaze was a fresh hit of pillowy softness. "Is it stress? Because of all you've been through?"

"Yeah." He was exhausted by it. Bone-deep tired. The desire to ask for solace with her was profound.

"I'll try not to get up in the night and disturb you, then."

Heh. Good luck with that, he thought as she went back into her room and closed the door.

"Hunter said that?"

"No. He was the only one encouraging me to stick with it, but I thought Neal and I would start our family right away so it made sense to focus on my marriage. Or so I thought. I was twenty. What can you expect?" she joked, trying to hide how much it still pained her that she'd quit for him. For a life that had been a pantomime of things she wanted, but false and farcical at its core.

"How long were you married?"

"Six years." She could have left it there, but she was tired of maintaining an illusion that she had been in love. "It was more of a merger than a marriage." She darted a look at him, expecting him to judge her again.

He only held his expression of polite interest.

"I'm not business-minded. Not like Hunter. Our father didn't really want me there anyway. He was all about the boys' club and father-son legacy. He was pretty sexist." Horribly sexist, actually. His attitude had been that women were good for a handful of things, most of them involving the way they were plumbed. "I thought if I married to benefit the business, Dad would be happy."

"He wasn't?"

"Not particularly. But I should have known

better. I should have listened to Hunter and stayed in school. He already had a connection with Dad, though. I didn't, but I wanted one. The thing I failed to realize was that *Dad* didn't want one. Not with me." It took everything she had to keep her voice even, but the unsteadiness was there, deep in her chest. "That's what I meant yesterday, when I said we'd had different upbringings."

He blinked in a small flinch, as though he couldn't imagine his father behaving so callously.

"And you don't have kids. Do you? I only mean, I didn't see anything online that suggested you had."

"No. No kids." The topic was still raw enough to catch in her throat. "Which I know people will say is a blessing once they hear we're divorced. No children were harmed by the breakdown of this marriage," she said with bitter humor. "It doesn't feel like a blessing, though."

"I stepped on a nerve. You wanted a family," he acknowledged grimly.

"I did. But I can't. I have what's called a hostile uterus."

"I've never heard of that."

"It means I can't get pregnant. Not without

help." She spotted the striped, mousy shape of a chipmunk scampering in the branches of a nearby tree. She started to block it onto her page. "That worked for Neal because he didn't really want kids."

It was the first time she'd said that aloud, always keeping that hurtful truth unspoken so it sat pulsing and festering under her skin, insult to the injury of her fertility issues. It was the reason she had asked him for a divorce the first time.

"He told me he wanted a family before we married, but he's the kind of salesman who will tell you anything to close a deal." She exchanged pale ivory for almond, working fast before she lost sight of the small creature.

"After we married, he kept talking me into putting it off. 'Don't do it to make your father happy'," she quoted. "It would have made *me* happy, but mutual consent, right? Finally, he agreed to try, but a year and a half went by without success. I was devastated every month. He was relieved. I could tell."

She scratched honey and umber against the page.

"I wanted to try IVF, but he had a lot of excuses for why the timing wasn't right and he kept missing his appointments."

She didn't look at Jasper, not wanting to see his reaction. He was probably turned off by her oversharing or giving her a look of pity, but silence was one more thing she had endured for the good of Wave-Com. She was so tired of suffering in silence.

Maybe she just wanted to justify her divorce since she felt so guilty about giving up.

"I finally faced that it was better if I didn't have children with a man who didn't want them. At the time, Dad had just died and Hunter was going through a court case with our stepmother, so I didn't tell him that Neal and I were separated. I wanted to keep it out of the press anyway. I started taking curating jobs in Toronto and spent most of my time there. Neal didn't care." She reached for hickory.

"It must have felt very unfair that Amelia got pregnant so easily."

"Everything about pregnancy is unfair. Now, at least, I'll be able to find someone who wants what I want." Antique brass. "Maybe I'll do it on my own."

"Single parenting is hard."

She dropped her pencil.

"That's not the voice of experience," he said dryly, catching the pencil as it rolled across the table toward him. "Maybe it is a little." He offered it back to her.

"What do you mean?" she asked as she took the pencil.

"Dad worked shifts while I was growing up. Even when he was home, he was often sleeping off his graveyard rotation. Mom ran the show. She came across as strict, but it was necessity, especially when Amelia was little. We were solid middle-class, not struggling, but no frills, either. Dad had a union wage as a tradesman. Mom worked at the sewing shop, but she literally could not do it all, so I picked up groceries and learned to cook and walked Amelia to the dentist after school."

"How old were you when you lost her?" she asked gently.

"I was finishing high school. I had been accepted at UBC, but I couldn't leave and come all the way across the country. Dad still had to work. Amelia was eleven—not old enough to stay home alone at night—so I stayed and provided some half-assed parenting while I took courses at the local college until I could transfer to U of T."

"Geology?" she guessed.

"And geography and business. I left when Dad made foreman and started working steady days. I did a couple years in the oil patch, then the Yukon, working on my master's degree. REM-Ex like to paint me as some upstart they hired off the street, but I had been operating as a private consultant for five years by then, building my professional reputation. They don't get to take that away from me."

The deadly promise in his tone sent a shiver down her spine.

"But you were talking about your ex," he reminded. "You said yesterday that you still have to inform him? When does that happen?"

"Any day." The chipmunk was gone, so she filled in what she could from memory. "He's in and out of the office. It's a matter of the process server catching up to him."

"Will he contest it?"

"I don't see how he can. We've been separated a year. I'm agreeing to exactly what was in our prenup. And, look, I want to say I'm sorry," she blurted, lifting her gaze so he could see her remorse. "Now that I understand why you're here, I can see what a nuisance it is that I showed up. I didn't mean to jeopardize what you're doing, but this seemed like the only way. I tried to end it once and Neal threatened to make it really difficult. He'll probably still make it difficult, but this time I'm not asking him for a divorce. I'm telling him. I can't stay tied to him. I just can't." The despondency that encased her when she thought of it was absolute.

"I understand," he said quietly. "You don't have to apologize for that."

"Thank you." She started sliding her pencils back beneath their loops, but couldn't seem to make her fingers cooperate. She wound up clapping the top of the box over the loose pencils and rising. "I'm going for a walk."

It started to rain while she was changing. She put off her walk and read a couple more chapters of high-seas sex.

By the time the rain let up, she was in dire need of cooling off. Sheesh! Too bad she wasn't a petite ballerina of a woman like the heroine. Jasper was strong, but she didn't think he could brace her high on a wall with his bare hands on her butt while he stood with his head buried between her thighs.

She kind of wanted to find out, though.

"Jasper, I'm going down to the beach," she called as she trotted down the stairs.

"I'll come." He closed his laptop.

"You don't have to." She turned at the bottom of the stairs to face him at his desk. She felt as though her dirty thoughts were right there at the forefront of her mind, still warm on her cheeks. Could he see them? "I just want some exercise."

"Me, too." He rose and stretched his arms up. His gaze slid down her jeans in a way that caused the embers of desire sitting in her belly to flare hotter.

He was checking that she was dressed appropriately, for heaven's sake. That's *all*.

The temperature had dropped significantly from yesterday, now that the tail end of a rainstorm was pushing inland, drawing cool air through the wet trees. She hugged herself in her pullover as he locked the basement door behind them.

"This is a weird situation," she said as they started down the path. "I feel like we're strangers on a train, both waiting to arrive at a new place in our lives. I want to make conversation to pass the time, but we keep falling into really heavy topics."

"Where are you headed?" he asked with dark humor. "Freedom? I'm going all the way to revenge."

"Oof." That just made her feel melancholy. "What if we did meet on a train, though? And our destination was Edmonton and none of this other stuff was happening? What would you talk to me about?"

"Rocks. That's why I'm still single."

She had to chuckle at that. "Really? Well, good news. I don't know anything about rocks. Why did you decide to study them?"

"I don't even remember. Dinosaurs, I think. There was a school trip to a place not far from where we grew up that got me excited about fossils. Looking for those is like gambling. You only need to find one trilobite and you're hooked for life. I started learning how they were made and that led me into geodes and stalagmites and diamonds. Pretty soon I needed to know where every kind of rock came from."

"The universe?" she joked.

"Time," he replied. "And the power of nature. The fact I can stand here and hold something that existed millions of years ago fills me with awe." He stopped and pointed at the ground. "In some ways, it's beyond comprehension, but it also makes me realize how small I am. How little I matter."

"There is a strange comfort in that, isn't there?" she said, captured by that thought.

"What would you talk to me about?" he asked curiously.

"Oh, I wouldn't talk to you." She shook her head. "I'd be too scared."

He dipped his chin. "I admit I've been in a very salty mood lately, but none of this has happened." He flicked his hand toward the house. "Tell me about your relatives in Edmonton."

"What makes you think I have relatives in Edmonton?"

"It's not exactly a hotspot for tourism. Unless you're going there for work? That's why I went there."

"I don't know why I'm going." She hugged herself as even this silly game devolved into something more serious. "I've never taken the time to figure out who I am, so I can't tell you." Dear Lord, that sounded tragic.

"You're single?"

"On the train? Yes," she said firmly.

"Maybe you're visiting a lover." His eyelids drooped with speculation.

Her heart lurched. "I don't think so."

"Why not?"

Because then she couldn't talk to him on the way there. Not like this, with possibility beginning to sparkle on the air between them.

Was she imagining it?

She nervously licked her lips.

His narrowed gaze followed the tip of her

tongue, making wanton urges seesaw in her stomach.

She nervously looked past him to where the path continued.

"We should talk about it," he said in a rumbling voice that was as low as a train car rattling over the tracks.

"What?" She flashed her attention back to his mouth and the way his lips shaped words. She pressed her folded arms to her middle, practically hunched into a ball of apprehension and yearning.

"About the fact that we're two people sharing a house, and whether that's all we'll share."

She opened her mouth, but her throat closed.

"That's not pressure or presumption on my part," he continued quietly. "Shake your head and we won't talk about it ever again."

She couldn't move. She was paralyzed with longing and fear of rejection.

For a few moments, there was only the drip of rain off the trees.

He stepped closer and watched his own finger as he scooped a tendril of hair that had fallen from her ponytail and tucked it behind her ear. His fingertip lingered on the shell of her ear, slowly tickling down to the hollow behind her earlobe and leaving a trail of fire against the side of her neck.

"*Is* it something you want to talk about?" he asked.

"I don't know how," she admitted in a strained whisper.

"Talk about? Or do?" The corner of his mouth dug in with humor while his finger traced her collarbone where it was exposed by the neckline of her pullover.

"D-do." Her eyelids fluttered at the sensation his barely-there touch was provoking. "I don't know how to be with anyone except—" She didn't want to say his name. Not right now. "I mean physically," she clarified, dying at how naked she felt. "Because I don't want to jump out of one commitment and into another, but I don't want to use you as a rebound."

"No?" All his fingers came into play as he caressed her throat. "I would love you to use the hell out of me right now."

She swallowed.

His hand cupped her throat, making her aware of how hard her pulse was pounding into his palm.

"What if it's awful? I don't want to sit across from you at Christmas dinner someday and remember how awkward this week was."

"It won't be."

"How do you know?"

Something perplexed and amused and patient sifted behind his eyes as he slid his hand to hook it behind her neck and slowly dipped his head. He barely grazed his mouth across hers, just enough to leave her lips buzzing with yearning.

Her eyelids fluttered closed and she reflexively took hold of the front of his sweatshirt, drawing him closer.

A rumble sounded. Thunder? No, it was a sound of satisfaction deep in his chest.

He continued to hold her for his lazy, teasing kisses. His mouth caught hers more deliberately. Once, twice…

She stopped breathing, aching with anticipation.

On the third pass, he shuffled his feet wider and set a heavy hand on her waist, fingers digging in. He slanted his head, unhurried while they found the right fit. She went up on her toes, increasing the pressure.

His arm went around her, then. He drew her tight against him. Secure. Then he devoured her until she was dizzy. Until she forgot that breathing was a thing and that anything beyond this seductive heat existed.

She stretched herself against him, curling her arm around his neck for balance, reveling in his hands moving over her back. Reveling in the thickness of his erection against her abdomen. She hadn't felt wanted in so long. Ever. Not really. But there was the proof. He wanted her.

She could have wept.

She kissed him back with abandon, falling into the bliss of it, distantly thinking, *This is how it's supposed to feel*.

Or not. With a rough growl, he twisted and set his arm against the rough trunk of a tree, then trapped her in the cage of it. While the exhale of the towering cedars soaked the air with their fragrance, his mouth came back to her in a deep, lush kiss. His free hand slid over the pocket of her jeans, long fingers splayed across the cheek of her backside, wicked and thrillingly possessive as he lifted her leg, guiding her to crook her knee to his waist where he trapped it with his elbow.

Now his hips pinned hers and that fierce evidence of his desire was flush against where she was soft and yielding. He rocked in a deliberate rhythm that sent shots of gold outward to her fingertips.

This was how it was supposed to feel. Like she was ripe and ravenous and divine.

His mouth caught her wanton sobs and his tongue brushed hers. She sucked on it and speared her hands into his hair and lifted her hips into that relentless pressure that was driving her mad. Climax was always elusive for her, but she'd never been this aroused. She was so close that she trembled.

His heady kiss abruptly stopped, leaving her mouth feeling abandoned and bruised.

She dragged open her eyes, dazed, bracing for a hard clunk back to earth if she was in this alone, but he wore a flush of carnal hunger on his cheeks.

"Feeling awkward yet?" he asked in a voice roughened by lust and smugness.

"I've never felt like this in my life."

He sobered. "You should always feel like this."

A stab of inadequacy had her looking to the base of his throat.

His hot mouth swept down into the crook of her neck and he nuzzled his way back to her ear where he let her feel the edge of his teeth.

"Come back to the house with me. Let me keep making you feel like this," he whispered.

She nodded and let him draw her back up the hill.

CHAPTER FIVE

THEY ENTERED THROUGH the basement where they removed their muddy shoes. Jasper hung his wet sweatshirt on a hook. Vienna did the same with her pullover, wavered briefly, then opened her jeans. The seat was damp from where he'd pressed her against the wet trunk of the tree and probably stained by the moss.

He watched very closely as she peeled them off and threw them onto the washer.

"Those are pretty." His touch was cooled by the outdoors, so goose pimples rose on her skin as he grazed the lace of her bikini-style undies across her hip and upper thigh.

"I—"

She sucked in her breath as the knuckles of his two bent fingers brushed the emerald silk down the center in a feather-light caress that made her throb.

"You do have trouble talking, don't you?" he teased as he dragged his gaze up to hers.

All she could see was the wall of his chest and the sinful tilt of his mouth and the promise in his eyes. With a shade more pressure, he drew a firmer line in the silk.

"I—" She tried to remember what she had to say. "I don't have condoms. I've had every test and I can't get pregnant, but—"

"There are some in the en suite bathroom."

She suddenly whirled away from him and ran to the bottom of the stairs leading up to the kitchen.

When she stopped there and looked back, he was in the open door of the laundry room, hands braced on either side of it.

"It's like that, is it?" His voice was gritty enough to tighten her hand on the stair rail. "You'd better run, then, because I'm definitely going to eat you."

A small scream left her as she raced up the stairs and through the pantry, tossing a look behind her when she reached the kitchen.

His steps resounded with steady purpose, oozing confidence that he would overtake her.

It was a thrilling chase that had her doing something wild because she felt wild. Unfettered. There were no wrong answers today, not with him.

She skimmed the lace and silk down her legs and left them at the bottom of the stairs as she started up them.

He swore as he emerged from the pantry and spotted them.

She laughed, starting to run again, but she was looking back, so she stumbled on the stairs.

He was there to catch her, softening her landing, his strength so far outmatching hers that he turned her in a way that felt as though she did it herself. Perhaps she did. Either way, she was pressed onto her back on these see-through stairs and he was braced over her.

"I want you like nothing I've ever wanted," he told her.

The faint stubble on his chin burned as he stole a hard kiss.

"And I have *wanted*, Vienna. For the last year, I have wanted a lot of things. All day and night, I made myself all sorts of promises if I could only get my life back. You, though… I didn't know I wanted you." His hand slid under her shirt, palming her breast through her bra while his teeth scraped the point of her chin.

"Then let's go upstairs," she urged. One stair tread was a sharp line in the middle of her back.

Her foot found another so she could lift and arch, alleviating the discomfort, but he was still heavy upon her.

"What did I just tell you I was going to do?" He dragged the hem of her shirt up and slid down to kiss her stomach, then he warmed her mound with a hot breath.

She groaned and tried to bring her legs together, but he was having none of that. He set his teeth against her inner thigh in warning and shifted so he could hug her legs while he knelt on a lower tread.

"Jasper." It was darned close to the pirate fantasy and— "Oh…" she gasped, as his tongue took a long taste of her, leaving a damp stripe of yearning in its wake.

She suffered a flash of *I don't deserve this*. She was supposed to absorb pain, not accept selfish pleasure, but his palm slid up, capturing her breast again while he painted those licks of acute sensation into her center.

Maybe she would have pushed him away if he hadn't made such a noise of gratification, but he acted as though she was offering him something, instead of selfishly enjoying it. Her hands didn't know where to settle. She wound up grasping through the stairs above her to find the back edge of a step. Now she was secure and able to arch her back off the corner of the stair so there was nothing but pleasure as she offered herself, his to consume.

He feasted on her with unhurried purpose, as though savoring her. As though the press of his finger into her was as much for his own pleasure as hers, despite the fact it made her flesh clench and quiver.

All her orgasms were self-induced. She had never been given one so generously, and suddenly she felt very vulnerable. Her thighs tried to close again, but one finger became two. The rhythm of his movement was slow and slick and drew her even closer to the edge of climax.

Her body moved of its own accord, hips lifting as she twisted in the agony of wanting him to keep pleasuring her this way while trying to maintain some semblance of herself. A bleak sense rose in her, warning that if she let herself go completely, he could break her.

The cracks and fissures were chasing her anyway, crumbling her ability to resist that final surrender. Her shivers became shudders. Her flesh clamped onto his intruding fingers and her orgasm accosted her with the force of a hurricane.

She rolled her hips as she rode out the buffeting waves, aware that the noises of abandon echoing off the rafters were coming from her, but she couldn't bite them back. This was too powerful to withstand. Too intense to bear.

Yet so very satisfying.

With her breaths still rattling her chest, she slowly relaxed.

He swept his tongue up to her still trembling abdomen, then pushed her bra cup out of the way and caught her nipple in his mouth. He lingered to draw on it, pulling forth fresh threads of need before he released it with a wet pop. Then he kissed her jaw and somehow gathered up her boneless body.

He carried her up the final stairs and into his bedroom. She was still dazed when he set her on the bed. In some belated reflex, she tugged the veil of her shirt down across the apex of her thighs.

His brow went up. The lazy heat in his expression banked. "Changing your mind?"

"No." She made herself release her shirt. "Shy."

She expected him to laugh at her. It was too late for bashfulness after that performance, but he only sent his gaze in a proprietary wander down her legs and back up to where her breasts lifted the front of her shirt.

"You have nothing to be shy about. I will

happily relive that memory every time I use those stairs."

"That's what I'm afraid of."

"Why?" He slipped into the bathroom and came back with a box. He pulled a condom from it and left both on the nightstand, then popped the button on his jeans.

He was dismantling her defenses with no effort whatsoever. A kiss, a caress, a heavy-lidded look and a rumble of approval in his voice.

She had always been very good at keeping a wall between herself and other people. She offered tiny pieces of her thoughts and ambitions, her emotions and her deepest insecurities, but always on her own terms.

She was afraid she wouldn't be able to hold herself back from giving everything to him. Actually, she had just let go of far more inhibitions than she had expected to. He was shaking her to her very foundations.

She *should* change her mind, but he was stripping off his shirt and pushing his jeans down and off, taking his underwear at the same time. He straightened in all his masterfully formed glory.

A very primitive part of her admired him as he tore open the condom and rolled it on. He was the epitome of a powerful, appealing mate, the kind who struck a sharp pang in her angry womb because it would never carry his baby. He would make beautiful babies and stick around to keep them fed while protecting them from lions and crocodiles, she just knew it.

As he came down over her, he seemed carved from golden heartwood, lovingly polished and hard, but deliciously alive.

"Still shy?" he asked as he nuzzled her temple. "Or can we lose this shirt?"

She touched his shoulder and he rolled away. She sat up and threw off her shirt, then unfastened her bra and dropped it off the edge of the bed, too.

When she sprawled herself over him, he drank in a long breath, chest lifting her while he ran his hands over her back, making her arch into him. Her legs fell open across his and she moved on him as they kissed, wanting the friction of his chest hair against her breasts.

"Bring those up to me." He cupped her bottom, urging her to rise and offer her nipples to his questing mouth.

It was blatant and again felt like a selfish move, but he seemed very happy to have her present herself this way and his attentions sent fresh arrows of need straight into her loins. She combed her fingers into his hair while he cupped and toyed with her breasts, drawing her nipples to sharp points until they were so sensitive she could hardly bear the texture of his tongue across them, but the ripple effects in her pelvis were worth it. Eager slickness gathered there until she felt hollow and lost. Until she needed the broad shape of him inside her. *Needed it.*

"Can we…?" She drew back, shifting backward and straddling him, taking hold of his steely shape, squeezing and caressing, learning how to make his breath catch before she guided him where she needed him. *There.*

She knew he was watching her. She closed her eyes against the intimacy, but that only amplified the sensation of his broad presence invading her. She slowly—gratefully—impaled herself upon him.

Oh, that felt good.

His hands never stopped moving, tickling her thighs and shaping her hips, clasping her waist and cupping her breasts then sliding down so his thumbs could bracket where they were joined. He parted her outer folds, found the moisture where she was stretched around him and caressed it all around her inner tissues. He rolled his thumb across the knot of nerves that made her clench her inner muscles and an earthy cry of pleasure lodged itself in her throat.

She began to move on him, greedy for the friction and the plunge. He rolled his hips, meeting her each time she returned. He drove her relentlessly upward until her hands were slipping on his sweaty chest.

It's okay, she wanted to tell him. *It won't happen for me. Not like this. But you should let go.*

She couldn't speak, though. Flames of acute pleasure were licking upward through her, lashing and twisting and pulling at her. Then one strong hand clasped her hip and held her still on his thrusting hips.

She began to shake. Maybe she already was shaking, but when he slid his other hand between them and pressed his thumb firmly on that swollen knot of nerves, her vision went white. Lightning struck, making her sob.

He rolled his thumb and lightning exploded all around her. Within her. Pleasure struck again and again with such ferocity that she didn't know if she could survive the storm. She didn't care. She was wind and rain and fire and light. She was shameless as she ground herself on him, greedy and unrestrained.

Then the world spun and he was atop her, thrusting powerfully. Whatever control he'd exerted until this point evaporated. Yet he didn't hurt her. He was near feral in his drive toward his own satisfaction. Ragged noises tore from his throat on each uneven thrust, but she only cried, "Yes. Yes." And when she opened her eyes to the lust suffusing his face, he was watching her. His teeth were bared, his hands clenched on her shoulder and hip, holding her still for his rough, animalistic claiming, but she was safe.

And wanted. *Needed*.

She had never felt so necessary. His focus told her she was his salvation and, impossibly, that knowledge caused a delicious wrenching inside her that brought her to the brink yet again.

She curled her nails against his ribs and begged, "Don't stop. Never stop."

His wordless noise was pure torture, but he kept thrusting. He didn't let go and didn't let up, not until her ragged breaths were broken by fresh cries and she was pulsing with the intense contractions of the joy he delivered so ruthlessly.

Only then did he bury himself deep and re-lease his own shouts of triumph.

Jasper gathered his weight off her and gen-tly pulled free, glad that Vienna kept her eyes closed because he needed a minute.

He needed a lifetime to process that. What the hell had just happened?

He rolled to the side of the bed where he discarded the condom in a wastebasket, then he fell onto his back.

Kissing her in the trees…he hadn't planned that. He had been very prepared for her to shoot him down when he floated the idea of them passing their time here with a pleasant hookup.

Maybe he had even hoped she *would* shoot him down. He loved sex, but he wasn't a horny teenager with no sense of consequence. Far from it. At that age, he had learned an indelible lesson on the responsibilities and consequences that could befall a man when he let his south pole do his thinking. As a result, he was very careful when he considered getting involved with a woman.

Getting involved with her wasn't the same as hooking up with a stranger. They would see each other again. Her concern about awkward dinners was legitimate.

But when she had asked, *What if it's awful?* he could have laughed. Their chemistry was obvious. Wasn't it?

One kiss. That was all he'd intended. He'd wanted to kiss her and show her their potential, but she had swiftly ignited, taking him right along with her into the conflagration.

That had been the most incredible sex of his life. Every point of contact with her had penetrated to his bones, awakening parts of him that had been asleep for years, long before he'd left for Chile. Places he had deliberately sanded off and forgotten about.

He hadn't expected that. He had expected physical fulfillment, obviously. Maybe a few of those awkward moments she'd been worried about since few couples got it right the first time. But that? He hadn't been able to make it up the stairs. Not without making a claim on her.

That was what had consumed him from their first kiss, though. He had never been the possessive type, but a primal need had compelled him to wipe out the memory of the previous *one* man in her life. Not for his ego. It had been more basic than that. He had needed her to be as deeply affected by him as he was by her.

Paradoxically, the more she gave herself up to him, the more he craved. Making her writhe and lose all inhibition had filled him with power and humble gratification. With hunger for more. The hunger was still there. Need. He wanted more.

What if it's awful?

What if it's unstoppable?

"I'm, um, going to go," she choked and sat up.

"Are you crying?" He sat up in a horrified lurch and caught her arm. "Did I *hurt* you?"

"No." Her feet swung off the side of the bed. She drew a pillow into her lap and hugged it. "I just feel so stupid."

"*Why?* Don't. That was really great sex, Vienna." Wasn't it? Had he been so lost in passion that he'd missed something?

"Yes, I know that, Jasper," she said with strident anguish. "And now I know how truly *awful* the sex was that I suffered through for *years*."

Ah, hell. He started to tell her he'd never experienced anything like this, either, but didn't think it would be any consolation for her. Her sorrow wasn't about the quality of their sex, but the broken dynamic of her previous relationship. The broken promises and her broken dreams.

"That wasn't on you," he reminded her.

"Yes, it was. I stayed with him! I asked him for it. I *begged* him to please make a baby with me." She hunched into the pillow and her shoulders began to shake.

He couldn't take it. He raked the covers down, then dragged her under them, spooning around her while she wept into her pillow.

Don't let him do this to you, he wanted to urge. But he only stroked her hair and pressed his mouth to her crown and held her tight.

Vienna woke alone, thank goodness. She was able to slip into her room for a quick shower.

Her skin felt every stinging drop while her cotton-headed brain formed only one thought. *What had she done?*

She didn't know how to process so much intimacy. Not just the nudity and the way she'd let Jasper touch her, or even the way she had regressed into some primitive form of herself. She had told him the worst, most miserable secret of her marriage and *cried* about it.

No one saw her cry. They denigrated her when she did.

Man up, Vienna, her father would say.

She can't take a joke, Irina would say with an eye roll.

Quit being so dramatic, Neal dismissed.

Even Hunter, with the best intentions, had always tried to fix things. *Don't cry. I'll talk to Dad.*

Jasper hadn't said anything like that. He had

wrapped himself around her like a protective shell and let her drain the poison from her aching heart.

How was she supposed to come back from that sort of exposure? She couldn't! He would forever know how utterly tragic her mistakes were. How grossly she had misled herself and how pathetically she had debased herself to a man who wasn't worth it.

She had honestly believed she could have casual sex with Jasper because sex with Neal had been functional and detached. She had never loved him, not really. In the early days, when he'd been courting and charming her, she'd been infatuated and called it love. She had tried very hard to love him while trying to make their marriage work, but for a long time now, she hadn't even liked him.

As for Jasper, she didn't know what she felt. She didn't know him well enough to be sure her instinctual liking and trust were justified. She knew he valued the truth. He had principles. He was a generous lover and—this was what really made her nervous—he knew how good he could make her feel. That gave him power over her.

Remaining detached from him now would be impossible. Even as she winced in embarrassment at the memory of him taking her apart on the stairs, libidinous heat tracked back into her loins, pulsing a guilty throb where his mouth had been, wanting that again.

Stop, she begged her wicked, wanton brain.

She left the shower and dried off.

Outside, the rain had rolled back in, bringing an early dusk and a comforting patter on the roof. She dressed in three-quarter yoga tights and a cozy tunic, then made herself go downstairs.

He was cooking again. *Help*.

Why did he have to be so incredibly hot and so incredibly thoughtful? He was moving with his casual efficiency, muscles shifting beneath his jeans and a forest green Henley that looked soft enough that hugging him would make her sigh with contentment.

"Hi," she said sheepishly.

He sent her a look that was remote and inscrutable, making her heart unexpectedly swerve.

"Your divorce is in the national headlines." He reached for an empty wineglass and set it on the island. "Your phone has been ringing." He nodded at the table.

"Oh." Her stomach plummeted. She looked

to where she'd left her phone with her art supplies.

"I thought you said it was off." He poured the crisp wine from yesterday into the glass and returned the bottle to the fridge.

"That's the new one," she murmured. It wasn't really a throwaway, either. It was a new-model smartphone that she had kept on and charged and *close* for this very reason. "If it's ringing, Hunter has the number. He'll want to talk to me."

This is it. It's done.

But it wasn't. Not really. She had miles to walk before it was finalized, but the bomb had been dropped. She stared at the phone with anticipation and dread.

"Are you going to tell him you're here?" Jasper sipped his own wine, expression impenetrable.

"Not if you don't want me to." She sat down on the far side of the table so her only backdrop would be the black windows behind her.

She drew a breath and collected herself, piling all her fears and misgivings behind a mask of *everything's fine*, then pressed the button.

Hunter answered on the first ring.

"—join you after I talk to her," he was saying before slamming his full attention through the screen and onto her. "Vi."

"Hi." She forced a bright smile. "What a gorgeous view." Blue-green water stretched behind him toward an island with a massive misshapen rock upon it. "How's the trip?"

"Great." He shrugged off the paradise that was Bora Bora, demanding, "Are you okay?"

"Of course." She was aware of Jasper blatantly eavesdropping and could hear him saying, *Don't lie, Vienna. I hate liars.*

"Vi." Hunter's frown scolded.

"I know. I'm sorry. I should have talked to you about it first so you weren't blindsided. Neal didn't want anyone to know we were separated, but he didn't want a divorce, either. This was the only way."

"Don't apologize. Tell me what you need from me." Hunter pitched his voice into a gruff gentleness she'd only heard once and very recently, when Peyton had bopped her brow against his chin and started to cry.

"That, actually." Vienna blinked, fighting the unsteadiness that accosted her vocal cords. "For you to tell me you're not disowning me." She tried to make it sound like she was joking, but the fear had been real. She bit her lip, unable to keep her chin from crinkling and revealing her distress.

"Never," he swore. "I'm worried about you, though. The press will come after you pretty hard and I'm not there—"

"No! This is why I did it while you were away, so you wouldn't be bothered by all of that. I'm handling it."

"You're never a bother, Vi," he insisted, in a way that abraded her nerves.

He wasn't trying to invalidate her feelings, but the net result was the same. She bit the corner of her mouth.

He looked disgruntled, as if he knew his abrupt words had stung and regretted it.

"Listen. I would be more upset if you stayed married to someone who was making you miserable." That was a nod to the person who was really to blame for how fragile her sense of self-esteem was.

Their father had stayed married to Irina despite constant scandals and affairs. She was the reason the Waverly name still went viral. She was finally out of their lives, though, remarried and living in Palm Springs, torturing some other hapless man and his family.

"Where are you?" Hunter asked. "Do you need extra security? What can I do from here?"

"Nothing. Really. The B-team will have been given my instructions. I'll check in with them shortly and I've already asked for a security detail when I head back to Toronto. For the moment, I'm perfectly fine."

"Don't go to Toronto. Stay with us. Or we could meet at the cabin. Are you in Calgary? I don't recognize what's behind you."

"I leave for Germany before you get back. Oh, you probably don't know. Quinn and Micah are getting married."

"Really." He took a moment to consider the news that Eden's best friend was marrying Eden's brother. "I could never figure those two out, but wish them well for me. Add our names to the gift."

She snorted. "I don't know if that's what the etiquette books advise, but okay."

Eden didn't seem to be holding a grudge against Amelia for destroying her wedding to Hunter, though. The one time Vienna had been able to catch up with her, Eden had sounded really happy that she had married Remy. The fact that Vienna had been invited to Micah's wedding told her Micah didn't blame her for Hunter's actions. Maybe Hunter and Amelia's well-wishes would be a nice gesture that would close out that episode once and for all.

"I'll release a statement of support right away," Hunter said, veering back to the business at hand. "Are you sure you don't want extra security right now? Where are you?" he asked again, clearly not letting it go.

"Can I keep it redacted for the moment?" She didn't glance at Jasper. "My lawyer knows where to find me if it becomes relevant. I don't trust this phone."

"This isn't a secure line, either," he grumbled, gaze lifting off screen. "And Amelia's waiting for me on the beach, so I should go. Call me for *anything*. You hear me?"

"I will. Give Amelia my love. And kisses for Peyton."

"She's covered in sand right now, so that's a big ask," he said dryly.

"I insist, then. And—" She hesitated, unable to remember the last time she'd told him this, but hearing how close Jasper and Amelia were made her wish for a better relationship with her brother. "I love you." She ran the words together.

He recovered quickly from his shock and offered a gruff, "Love you, too, Vi. I'm always behind you. I hope you know that."

"I do." She was even starting to believe it. "Bye."

CHAPTER SIX

VIENNA CLEARED HER throat after she ended the call, visibly moved by her brother's support.

Jasper brought her wine to her.

"Thanks," she murmured as she sipped.

"Did you really think he would object to your divorce?" He was still astonished by that.

"No?" She grimaced. "Hunter has never let me down, but he's deeply invested in the company, emotionally and financially. He fought hard to pry Irina's fingers off it and is still repairing the damage she did. I've always seen my role as support. I'm supposed to make things easier for him, not harder."

By staying married to a man who had lied to her about one of the basic building blocks of marriage…? Either you wanted children or you didn't. There was nothing wrong with either choice, but partners had to agree because there wasn't much room for compromise in a game changer like that.

"I should check in with my PR team. It's a secure connection, don't worry."

He waved at her to go ahead and went back to the lemon pesto chicken he was throwing together.

When he'd woken with her in his arms, he'd still been reeling from how profoundly she was affecting him. He was a normal person who cared about people in an abstract sense. He wanted human rights for all and a clean planet and regularly gave to crowdfunding and emergency response charities and blood donation clinics. He would help an old lady cross a street, but the only people he really cared about—the people he would take a bullet for—were his father and sister. And niece, obviously. Saqui's family, too, he supposed.

He was starting to feel protective of Vienna, though, which didn't make sense given how recently he'd met her. He had been tempted to stay in bed with her, not simply for the sensation of her naked warmth snug against him, but because he wanted to *know* she was safe and warm and comforted.

Disturbed by that realization, he had slipped

away and come downstairs, where his idle glance at the headlines had jolted him.

She hadn't been wrong to hide from the coverage. That had been his first thought. He'd been skeptical of the lengths she'd gone to, escaping to a secret home and having her husband served his papers in her absence. It had seemed like a lot of subterfuge for something that was fairly routine in this day and age.

Not for a Waverly, apparently. The headlines were disgustingly sensationalized, none of them flattering or empathetic to a woman who simply wanted to leave a bad relationship. Notably, her husband wasn't vilified. He was barely mentioned. No, she was the focus and it was all slanted to tear her down.

Appalling as those stories were, there had been a part of him that was relieved to see her divorce made public, given he'd left her sleeping in the bed they'd wrecked. It was that primitive possessiveness rising in him again.

She's not his. That man doesn't deserve her.

And you do? a cynical voice asked him, deep in his psyche.

A chill wafted through his chest and he dismissed it. Vienna had made clear that she wasn't looking for another committed relationship. He wasn't in a position to offer one, either, so this affair—light and temporary—was a win-win.

If his circumstances were different, though…

They weren't, he reminded himself. He was fighting to get his life back and she was clawing her way into a new one. The broader question was, would this affair continue now that she was facing all she did?

"No, I don't need to hear what they're saying," she said with a strained smile. "I can imagine."

"Okay, but the fact that no one's seen you is becoming a story of its own," a woman on-screen was saying. "My concern is that Mr. Briggs might dox you."

"Neal has no idea where I am," Vienna said confidently. "Continue with the statements about requesting privacy and release whatever Hunter sends you. I hate to wish anyone ill, but isn't there a politician with his nose in the trough whose exposure could take some heat off me?"

The other woman laughed. "I'll see what I can find."

They signed off and Vienna released a shuddering breath. For one second, her expression was both haunted and hunted. How had he seen her as shallow? She felt things very deeply. She was too damned sensitive for a marriage based on business. Had no one seen that? Why hadn't anyone tried to stop her? Why hadn't Hunter?

She glanced self-consciously at him, then straightened her face and shoulders and spine.

"Everything's under control," she assured him with a bland smile. "Can I help with dinner? It smells delicious."

"No, it's ready if you are."

The food was delicious, but Vienna could hardly swallow. The silence between them felt thick and heavy. Sticky as tar.

When she found the courage to lift her gaze, she found Jasper watching her over the tilt of his wineglass.

The lump of food in her throat turned to stone. She washed it down with her own wine.

"I can't imagine what you think of me," she said in a voice scored by the tang in the wine.

"I think you're someone who wants more for herself and I can't help admiring that you're going after it, despite what you're up against."

"Really?" She searched his flinty expression, finding it far easier to believe that he would look down on her than up. "I thought you'd be wishing you'd never met me." *Or touched me. Or held me.*

All they'd done rushed back into her thoughts, making her cheeks sting.

"Not at all. But I can't help wondering if you'll wish you hadn't met me, once the dust settles." Something shifted behind his eyes, too indefinable for her to properly catch. "I'm happy to be your port in a storm, but I don't want to take advantage of you during a vulnerable time."

Her heart took a leap and a dip.

"I'm not vulnerable." She reflexively rejected any label that suggested she was weak. She couldn't afford to be. Ever.

His brows went up, skeptical. Was that slow blink of his patronizing? Pitying? The way he was focused on her gave her the sense he saw right through her. Almost as if he saw her more clearly than she saw herself. It was disconcerting.

"Vi. Can I call you that? I like it." He set his glass aside.

She nodded jerkily, even though it was a short form only people very close to her were allowed to use.

"I want you to be honest with me. I really do. But if you choose not to be, I can't stop you. Be honest with yourself, though."

She sucked in a breath, one that entered her

chest like a blade. Inexplicably, fresh tears arrived behind her eyes.

"You told me today that you don't know who you are. Start by acknowledging what's true. You're not hiding here because you're a coward. You've made a really tough decision to leave the life you had, knowing you'd be attacked for it. You're *vulnerable*. If you can't acknowledge that, then I'm definitely taking advantage of you."

She was so disconcerted by his assessment she could have sobbed.

"I'm not allowed to be vulnerable," she said on a soft cry. "I'm not allowed to be anything." Didn't he realize that?

That was the crux of it, though, wasn't it? She had spent her life trying to be what she thought others wanted her to be, rarely letting her true self into the light. When she had, she'd been mocked for it.

"What if you don't like who I am?" she asked in a near whisper. She couldn't take that kind of rejection. That was why she wore all these layers, so the scoffs and dismissals weren't really a rejection of *her*. She definitely couldn't take that depth of rejection from *him*.

She had already revealed a lot to him, though.

Things no one else knew. And he was still here, saying that he wanted to be her port in a storm.

"I want…" Oh, it was hard to give voice to her desire. It was an even greater risk now than it had been a few hours ago, when she had still thought she could have a fling with him and keep possession of herself. That wasn't possible at all now. She knew that, but she still wanted to be with him. If he rebuffed her after she worked up the courage to say so, she'd be crushed.

She tried to swallow, but her throat was too dry.

"I'm really scared," she admitted. "All I could think about was getting out of the cage, not realizing how much protection those bars offered. If I were here alone right now, I would be drowning in bleak terror. Maybe I would have lost my nerve and not gone through with the divorce. But you're here and…and you're showing me what I can have if I believe I deserve it. I really want to keep sleeping together. If you do."

The blue in his eyes turned to the heart of a flame.

"I do. I very much do."

Jasper had never taken ayahuasca, but making love with Vienna had to be what a hallucinogenic trip felt like. His senses were acute, making each touch and moan and taste that much more intense.

Vienna was right here with him, the connection between them exactly that: a connection. They occupied a plane of synchronicity where she seemed to know that the swirl of her tongue exactly *there* was precisely what he needed. That the sweep of her hair across his stomach would both soothe and incite him. She knew when it was time to roll beneath him with exquisite welcome because he was going to die if he wasn't inside her.

This was life at its most basic. Everything made sense when he was thrusting into her, lost to the magnificent, addictive madness. Her orgasm was swift and sharp and so powerful, it could have been his own.

He dragged her fist from his hair and scraped his teeth on the heel of her palm, waiting for her eyes to flutter open before he sealed his mouth over hers again, all of him screaming at himself to capture and conquer and *keep*.

He couldn't. The sheer power of this desire for her told him they were a dangerous combo, but he couldn't get enough of her. Even as her lips softened and parted beneath his, he withdrew so he could feast on the banquet of her.

"Where are you going?" She clawed at him, grimly sweet in her panic.

"Here," he rasped, sliding down so he could worship her breasts. "Everywhere."

Soon she would leave and he wouldn't have this. The sense of a clock ticking made him urgent and greedy. Demanding. He ran his mouth everywhere on her trembling body, until she was once again making those helpless noises that sent pleasurable shivers down his back.

"I can't bear it…" she gasped.

"What's wrong?" he crooned, rising over her again, cupping her cheek and pressing a tender kiss to the corner of her mouth.

"I need you inside me. So much." There was something chagrined in her pleading gaze.

"Take me, then."

Her hand slid between them, guiding him to sink back into her.

He shuddered with pleasure. His heart began to slam in his rib cage. He wanted to envelop her. Crush her. A flood of thick heat threatened to burst from him as he plunged into her molten core once more, now with more power. More need.

This isn't real, he insisted to himself.

Their response to each other was heightened by their isolation and their strange circumstances. They had been thrown into the same lifeboat and were clinging to each other out of desperation.

But when her nails curled against his skin and her breath broke, when her thighs clamped to his hips and she clenched around him like a fist, he reached the limit of his self-discipline. He abandoned control and thrust unevenly, taking her with him as he launched them both into oblivion.

Jasper swore, stiffening atop her even while Vienna was still enjoying the floaty afterglow.

They'd come back to bed after breakfast—or rather, she'd been admiring his physique while sketching him and he'd swooped the way a raptor snatches up a bunny. She still felt as though she was soaring.

He wasn't so mellow, though. He withdrew with less than his usual tenderness, setting an apologetic touch on her thigh when she flinched.

"What's wrong?" she asked.

"The condom split."

"Really? How old are they?"

"I never checked. I should have." His expression was grim as he shifted to sit on the side of the bed while he discarded the broken latex.

He stayed there gripping his knees, profile forbidding.

"Jasper." She touched his spine. "I can't get pregnant," she reminded, not bothering to hide the anguished pang in her throat. He knew this about her, the longing and the disappointment. It was who she was. "I've had every test you can imagine. There's nothing for you to worry about unless…?"

"I had a physical before I went to Chile. I haven't been with anyone except you." He looked over his shoulder, brows lowered in consternation.

"Then it's not a problem. Is it?"

He didn't look reassured, but his hands relaxed slightly. He restlessly swept them up and down his thighs as he looked forward again. "No. I guess it's not."

A cool breath of premonition lifted the hairs on the back of her neck. She opened her mouth, not sure what she needed to ask, but he rose abruptly.

"I'm going to shower."

He didn't invite her to join him, she noted with a pang, so she didn't follow him. She went to her own room, pensive as she pulled on a sundress.

This affair was thrilling and wonderful and

temporary, she reminded herself. It needed to remain a physical thing, not become an emotional relationship. Not deeply emotional, anyway. Jasper could easily take over her life if she let herself fall for him.

She probably would anyway, she realized with a wobbly sensation inside her. She was already wondering if he would ask her to come back here after she went to Germany. He hadn't said anything more about his plans for Orlin Caulfield and REM-Ex, but it was very clear that he would lie in wait as long as he had to. It bothered her that he was here all alone.

She wondered if there was anything she could do for him while she was away. She would have to ask him because people like Micah Gould and Remy Sylvain were as well-connected and powerful as Hunter. Maybe they could help.

A crunch of gravel outside had her dropping her hairbrush to peek out the window she had left open to let in the night air.

An SUV parked where the late morning light penetrated the trees and painted the driver in dappled spots as he stepped from behind the wheel.

Neal? What the hell!

She could hear the water still running in the

en suite, but didn't yell to Jasper, not wanting Neal to hear her talking to anyone. She flew down the stairs, rushing out the front door to meet her ex on the walkway to the front doors.

Neal Briggs had the handsomeness of a man with wealth—not classically good-looking, but polished and tailored to highlight his assets, the primary one being his money. His gym membership went mostly unused, but he skied and golfed to keep his weight down. He saw his barber monthly, paid his dentist to keep his teeth white, and kept his jaw shaved clean. He bought a new suit every season, but today was dressed casually in knee-length shorts and a green polo shirt with a designer logo on the pocket.

"Hello, darling." He removed his aviator sunglasses in a move she was sure he'd been practicing since seeing his first action star do it, back when he was twelve.

"How did you find me?" she demanded.

"My heart led me to you, of course." He spoke through a grimly satisfied smile.

She had never been afraid of him. He was a man who got what he wanted by saying what he had to, but she faltered briefly as she realized he was incredibly angry.

"I'm serious." She stood taller. "I want to

know how you found me. Did Steven tell you?" If so, Hunter's assistant was very freaking fired.

"Mr. Chow remains loyal to the crown, don't worry. No, I bought some handy little stickers last year. They help you keep track of things that are easily misplaced." Neal held up his phone.

"You *tracked* me?" She had removed a tile tag from her keychain before coming away, but it hadn't occurred to her to go through her luggage or purse looking for devices that Neal might have planted. Her brain exploded over how invasive this was. "That is stalker level awful, Neal."

"Relax," he scoffed. "I wouldn't have had to use them if you had told me where you were going, would I?"

"I don't have to tell you where I'm going! We are separated. *Divorcing.* Kindly get back in your car and drive out of my life or I'll call the police."

It was a bluff. Her thoughts immediately leaped to Jasper. She couldn't actually call the police. That would risk exposing him.

Neal saw her falter and snorted, mistaking her hesitation for a lack of mettle.

"Nice try, but we are not divorcing, Vienna. We had a good thing going with living apart and I'm willing to continue that, after our very public reconciliation, of course. Let's go inside and talk about how this will play out." He crowded up to her, trying to scoop his arm behind her back to bring her with him toward the front door.

She shoved his hands off her, pushing away and coming up against the rail on the walkway. Her reaction only allowed him to slip right by her into the house.

"Get. Out," she demanded.

"Who rented this place for you?" He glanced at the desk where Jasper's laptop sat closed and charging. "Chow? Hunter? I couldn't find anything on your credit card statement."

"*My* card?" She had opened new ones and hadn't used their joint accounts in months. "How do you even have access to that?"

He sent her a pitying look over his shoulder. "I know your mother's maiden name and the first concert you attended."

Ugh. All those times when he'd actually seemed to be interested in her had just been a fishing expedition?

"I'll tell my lawyer about this." She was growing more revolted by the minute at how closely Neal had been monitoring her activities. She was also sickly aware of Jasper upstairs.

What if he started rattling through drawers and Neal heard him?

Neal looked toward the kitchen and paused.

"That's two coffee mugs." He swiveled his gaze the other direction. "And a pair of really big shoes." Slowly he lifted his gaze to the top of the stairs. And went very still.

Vienna's insides congealed.

With horror, she watched Jasper's bare feet appear through the peekaboo stairs, unhurried as he descended into the cesspool that was her dissolving marriage.

CHAPTER SEVEN

As HE STEPPED from the shower, Jasper heard the chime of the front door opening. Voices. Vienna sounded angry. Distressed.

He stepped into a pair of shorts and yanked up the fly, hearing her cry, "You *tracked* me? That is stalker level awful, Neal."

Neal? A ball of hatred coalesced in his gut.

"I'll tell my lawyer about this." The shaken edge on Vienna's voice took him to the top of the stairs in time to see a crisply dressed man halt below and take note that she wasn't alone.

Jasper's plans for Orlin Caulfield and REM-Ex, delicate as a house of cards, flashed in his mind's eye as he met the affronted gaze of Vienna's ex.

"Who the hell are you?" Neal asked as Jasper descended the stairs, shirtless and shoeless and never breaking eye contact with this A-grade piece of garbage.

Was he infuriated that his plan for justice was suddenly in grave jeopardy? Oh, yes. But he wasn't going to leave Vienna to face this jackass alone.

"Everything all right, Vi?" Jasper paused on the bottom step.

"You didn't have to come down. Neal is leaving." She was clinging to her elbows, cheekbones standing out like tent poles holding up the distressed hollows of her cheeks. Her pleading eyes said, *I'm sorry.*

"Wow." Neal shoved his hands in his pockets, looking between them while wearing a calculating expression. "I genuinely didn't think you had it in you, sweetheart. You do recall there's an adultery clause in our prenup? Big brother put that in."

"I remember." Vienna's chin came up. "I remember why, too."

"*I* have stayed faithful since our wedding." He set a hand on his chest as though insulted she would suggest otherwise. "You can take that to the bank. Actually, *I* will, since you haven't."

"You can't claim adultery when we're separated," she said crossly.

"We'll see if the courts agree."

"Oh, go ahead. Run up the lawyer bills!" She flung her hand in the air. "I don't care."

"But what will the *papers* say?" He was enjoying toying with her. Jasper could see it and wanted to punch that smug glee right off his face.

"She didn't leave you for me," Jasper said flatly. "She simply left. *You*."

Neal didn't know what to make of that. His jaw worked as he held Jasper's stare, then his eyes narrowed. "I know you."

And there it was. Vienna had said he was in sales. People successful in that field tended to remember faces and names.

"You're Amelia's missing brother."

The pyramid of cards began to topple.

"That's going to play *really* well with the shareholders," Neal said to Vienna. "You left your husband for an affair with your brother-in-law? The one who's on the run for…what the hell is it you've done?"

Jasper stepped off the stair and would have stomped on Neal's foot if the other man hadn't stumbled backward in fear.

"Touch me and that's assault," Neal stammered.

"You came into this house uninvited. You're making threats against the occupants. I think it would be ruled self-defense. Would you like to find out?"

Neal curled his lip, but he had the heart of a coward. With fading bravado, he edged toward the door.

"I'll leave you lovebirds." He sent a smarmy smile at Vienna. "Buckle up, darling. It's going to be a bumpy ride."

As he walked past her, she spat two words that were not very ladylike, but under the circumstances, completely appropriate.

Shaken, Vienna watched to be sure the SUV left, then turned back to see Jasper wearing a thunderous expression.

Her stomach rolled sickly.

"He put trackers in my things." She couldn't even begin to imagine where all she would have to look. Luggage? Makeup? "That's criminal, isn't it?"

Knowing Neal, he would claim it had been a husbandly gesture, that he was tracking property, not her. She doubted it would go very far with law enforcement, but her skin was crawling.

"You didn't have to come down," she continued as Jasper's forbidding silence plucked at her overwrought nerves. "Let him see you, I mean. I could have…" She didn't know what she could have done. Picked up her keys and left? What if Neal had walked through the house and met Jasper upstairs anyway?

She had been so confident last night when she'd told her team that Neal had no idea where she was! All that careful planning and, instead of avoiding a feeding frenzy in the press, she'd made it worse. For both of them.

"He'll dox me. He might be posting something right now. We can't stay here." She could have cried. An hour ago, they'd been making love. Happy. "I'm so sorry, Jasper."

"So am I," he said grimly.

It's not my fault, she wanted to cry. Wasn't it, though? If she had just stayed in her suffocating little box of a life, not reaching for more, she wouldn't have caused him to be discovered. She'd ruined his plans. His life could be in danger!

"I have to make some calls," she said, lurching into damage control by searching for her phone. If she hurried to clean up the mess she'd made, maybe Jasper wouldn't hate her so much. "I have to inform Hunter and my lawyer. I'll ask the B-team to make a statement right away. We only have one chance to get ahead of whatever Neal might say. We'll say he's making more of this than it is," she asserted, having played the spin game many times with her stepmother's antics. "Relatives are allowed to stay in the same holiday house. There's nothing more between us than casual acquaintance."

She'd left her phone outside on the deck.

When she came back in with it, Jasper hadn't moved. He looked even more severe than he had when she'd first turned up here as his unwanted houseguest.

"I'm—" She had to clear a catch of dryness in the back of her throat. "I'll have my team arrange flights and security for us."

The adrenaline in her system ought to be making her feel stronger and faster. Fight. Flee! Instead, her arms and legs were growing sluggish and heavy. Her brain was turning to mush, sinking into a swampy darkness so she had to fight to keep breathing.

As Jasper stood there looking like he was cast in bronze, still and cold and hard, she heard her presumption in that word "us".

A tearing schism left her split and off-center. Her heart was on the floor as she hugged herself defensively.

Don't be needy, she scolded herself. She'd known they didn't have a future and this was why. She was a liability. The sex had been sex, nothing more.

"I feel responsible for breaking your cover," she said shakily. "I would like to mitigate the damage if I can. Tell me what you need and I'll have my team provide it."

His reply was a choked noise that could have been insult or lack of trust or sheer disbelief at how thoroughly she had compromised him.

She swallowed, but the hard lump in her throat remained.

"If you would prefer to do your own thing…" *Then I will feel like a discarded piece of trash.* She would *look* like trash, once Neal went public with his infidelity accusations.

Why did Jasper have to be her brother-in-law? It was *so* sordid. She wanted to curl up in a ball, but that was never an option. No, her dirty laundry always had to be on the line for all to see. Her only option was to walk forward through the gauntlet of shame. Again.

"Call Hunter," he said gruffly. "Make sure Amelia and the baby are protected. I'll call my father and make my own arrangements."

She didn't blame him for distancing himself, she really didn't, but she felt steeped in poison as his words filled her ears.

She nodded jerkily. "I'll leave as soon as possible."

She was gone thirty minutes later.

Jasper told himself that was good. His preference was to navigate this alone, as he had done for most of his adult life. It wasn't because he didn't want to involve himself in Vienna's divorce drama, although he didn't—yet he already had, he acknowledged grimly. Not that he had any regrets in how he'd handled Neal. If anything, he hadn't been hard enough on him. He should have scared him off for even glancing at Vienna ever again.

No, his far greater concern was that a public acknowledgement of their involvement could put her in the same jeopardy he and his family faced. He had already been thinking they should deny their relationship and part ways as quickly as possible when she had said, *There's nothing more between us than casual acquaintance.*

That had slid with unexpected abrasion across a very old wound, one that shouldn't still be so raw, but was.

In those seconds, as she offered to put her *team* at his disposal, as if he couldn't afford his own flight and security detail, he'd flashed back to a very well-dressed woman in a Lexus pulling up beside him as he was doing cart returns at the grocery store. She had introduced herself as his girlfriend's aunt and offered an upscale shopping bag with string handles. It had contained his hoodie, his favorite book on mineral identification, and the empty keychain that read *Sweet*, matching the fob on his own keys that read, *Heart*.

Your things, the woman had said. *Annalise is staying with me while she finishes school.*

But what about—?

His heart had thrust itself into his mouth.

She's seen the broader picture of her future. It doesn't include becoming a mother right now. Or you. Don't contact her.

Her body, her choice. Jasper had respected that. Given the still fresh loss of his mother and his crushing responsibilities to his father and sister, he'd been in a panic as to how he would also support a partner and a baby, but he felt no real comfort in having all of that yanked away. Especially not when the disdain in that woman's face left him feeling so inadequate and unworthy.

Her future doesn't include you.

Like he was some kind of war criminal. Annalise hadn't changed schools to avoid gossip. She hadn't wanted to see *him*.

And there was Vienna dismissing their relationship just as dispassionately, now that her association with him had consequences.

With bile sitting in the back of his throat, he

had carried her bag to the garage and nodded curtly when she said goodbye.

He didn't dwell on her abrupt departure. He had his own vehicle and his own crisis to manage, which was where he forced his thoughts to turn.

After a brief call to his father, warning him to take precautions, he called his lawyer to advise that he was moving his timeline up. He might not catch Orlin Caulfield in his net, but he could still snag a lot of slippery fish.

He packed as he made his next call, requesting his financial advisor reactivate all his accounts. Most of his holdings had been moved into trusts while he'd been missing. Amelia had been able to do that much, which had turned out to be a genius move, protecting his crypto balance when the rest of the world's had crashed.

He'd been using some of those funds to buy up REM-Ex shares under a shell company, but that was hardly the extent of his investments. Jasper had always had a leg up when it came to reading a feasibility study for a mining venture. He'd been growing his portfolio from his university days and could easily leverage what he held into whatever cash he might need for a flight. Or to purchase a private jet, if it came to that.

Vienna didn't know what kind of resources he had at his disposal because he hadn't told her. His father and sister probably didn't even know the extent of it. He preferred to live simply, rather than throw his money around, but he had plenty of it. That early experience of not being good enough had driven him to work hard and prove he *was* good enough.

Then Orlin Caulfield had cut short the life of his friend as if Saqui was unimportant. He'd tried to sacrifice Jasper in the same way, all to hang on to his own riches.

Jasper loathed that level of arrogance and kind of despised himself that he had felt so compelled to rise—sink?—to the same affluent level. At least it meant he could make Orlin choke on his misapprehensions.

Or could have, if he'd been able to wait until Orlin was back. *Damn it.*

His last sweep of the house for his own belongings took him outside where fat raindrops had begun to plonk on Vienna's sketchpad.

Stand there, she had insisted this morning— had it only been this morning?

He'd watched the dreamy look that transformed her face as she moved her pencils, fluidly exchanging one color for another, bringing her gaze back to him again and again.

It had been erotic, standing there unmoving while her eyes traveled over him so thoroughly. When he was so hard he couldn't stand it, he'd stolen the pad from her hands and carried her up the stairs.

He was making more of their affair than it was, likening their lovemaking to a drug trip that had left him fundamentally altered. They'd come together at a time of heightened pressure. Releasing that pressure had felt inordinately good. *That's all.*

He studied her sketch. It was undeniably good, but unsettling. Revealing, even, which caused an itch behind his sternum. It was him, but it was an image of himself he didn't recognize. Had he really packed on that much muscle? He wasn't one to preen in front of a mirror, especially once he'd seen how wasted he'd been after a year of trading farm labor for meals and a bed.

He'd been eating three squares since arriving here and worked out downstairs every day, mostly to relieve tension and try to exhaust himself toward sleep. He hadn't noticed that his T-shirt was sitting so snugly against his skin, though.

The perspective against the rail, with the treetops below and behind him, made him seem bigger than he was. Her faint blocking lines gave him the suggestion of an invisible suit of armor, too, increasing the impression that he was strong. Powerful.

It was strange to see himself like that when he'd spent a year feeling like quarry, hamstrung and outgunned.

This was the ambitious man he'd been before he'd left for Chile, the one who had been confident in who he was, but it exposed how he'd also become harder. Hardened.

A splat of rain landed on the pensive line of his mouth, snapping him out of his introspection.

He took the pad and pencils into the house, thinking to leave them on the table, but when he carried his things out to the garage, the sketchpad was among them.

One week later, Jasper stood outside the REM-Ex boardroom, flicking through his phone while he waited for the board to assemble themselves.

"What you're seeing are the actions of a disgruntled ex," Vienna had said of Neal's accusations when she held a press conference shortly after she had left Tofino. "I can't and won't speak for Mr. Lindor except to confirm that he and I were staying in the same summer house for the same reason. We both wanted privacy during a difficult time."

Neal had then gone ahead and revealed Vienna's infertility. According to Amelia, Vienna had promptly lashed back by having Neal fired from Wave-Com for breaking a nondisclosure agreement regarding family privacy. He'd lost all his perks in one swoop, including his condo, company car, and cell phone.

Jasper was grimly proud of her for going full scorched earth on the bastard.

Now she was in Germany, where photos were emerging of her at a lavish wedding. It was held at some fancy palace hotel and every snapshot showed her smiling and beautiful. Different. She wasn't the woman who had padded barefoot through the house, hair in a low ponytail, face clean of makeup. She wore elegant gowns and diamonds in her ears. A man in a tuxedo— Remy Sylvain, the caption read—stood with his arm around her while they beamed at each other with unmistakable affection.

Not his business, Jasper assured himself, clicking off his phone and ignoring the churn of gravel in his gut.

Vienna had moved on. Fine. He had no quarrel with that. They'd made no promises to each other.

But it ate at him.

"Sir? Everyone is present," his new executive assistant informed him.

Not everyone. Orlin Caulfield, President of REM-Ex, was beaming in via video conference along with a handful of other board members. He scoffed the second Jasper was introduced.

"*You're* Keady Holdings?" Orlin said of the company Jasper had formed on his return to Canada. "I knew something was off when I couldn't find anything about the company that's been buying up our shares these last weeks. This is not an acquisition offer, gentlemen. It's an HR dispute. Meeting adjourned."

"This *is* an acquisition offer," Jasper said firmly, not bothering to take a seat. "Since the board is legally required to consider all serious offers, stick around."

"How serious could you possibly be?" Orlin scoffed.

Jasper named a share price that had everyone sitting up and looking at one another.

"The shareholders will want to hear about that, won't they?" Jasper said knowingly. "I'm not attaching a lot of strings, either. My only condition is an environmental audit going back for the last five years. And an independent investigation into Saqui Melilla's death."

Figuring out who were the rats on this particular ship was as easy as watching which faces turned to stone. A couple of the remote screens went black.

"This is a stunt," Orlin charged. "You're about to find yourself in the middle of a very grave safety violation. One that could end in criminal charges."

"No, Orlin. You are." Jasper leaned on the table and looked at the ring of uncomfortable expressions around him. "I strongly suggest the board remove this liability from the helm. Immediately. If you don't, I will fire him the minute I'm in charge. I assume that those of you with nothing to hide will support my takeover and the ensuing investigations. As a one-time offer, I will allow anyone worried about what might crawl out from under a rock to quit the board, sell your shares to me, and flee to a country without extradition agreements. Those who want to fight me had better have the capital to back up the legal bills. I sure do."

He could see the bluster bleeding out of everyone as he spoke. They were all looking to each other and casting uncertain glances at the stony-faced Orlin.

"Do we need a special resolution?" Jasper pressed. "All in favor of selling the company to Jasper Lindor, raise your hand. I think that's two thirds, isn't it?" He said to his assistant as they counted the votes. "Bring in the rest of my team. Let's close this deal."

CHAPTER EIGHT

VIENNA HAD BEEN home from Germany for more than two weeks, but couldn't seem to shake her jet lag.

She'd been going through a lot, she reminded herself. It was natural that she would have a hard case of the blues, but she had weathered bad press and bruised feelings before. This was different. She was heartsick over Jasper and the way things had ended between them.

He seemed to have landed on his feet. In a press conference he declared, "Given how my friend and interpreter, Saqui Melilla, was killed, I feared my own life was in danger. Now that I'm back in Canada, I'm looking forward to working with REM-Ex to find who was really responsible for Saqui's death and hold them accountable."

With that hand grenade thrown firmly back into REM-Ex's court, Jasper had proceeded to *buy the company* in a hostile takeover, forcing an independent investigation, the kind they should have performed in the first place. According to reports, he'd been an early adopter of cryptocurrency and had quietly made a fortune that he had rolled into mining investments through the years. The REM-Ex board approved his purchase and installation as president *because* he was revealed to be so successful in their field.

Orlin Caulfield was ousted without ceremony and was quoted as being "very concerned" and "cooperating fully." He was also still out of the country. Vienna knew it must gall Jasper that the man was literally getting away with murder.

And whose fault was that? *Hers*.

With a whimper, she threw her arm over her eyes where she lay on the couch.

The guilt was killing her, but it was exacerbated by the knowledge that Jasper would never forgive her for ruining his plan. If they had managed to keep their relationship under wraps, they could have at least parted as friends. Maybe, at some later time, they might have come together again, but that was never going to happen now. She doubted he would so much as give her the time of day.

She was so mortified and agonized over what

she'd done, she couldn't even face him. Amelia had invited her to come visit and Vienna had demurred, making excuses because she knew Jasper was living in Vancouver. She didn't want to see him.

She didn't want to see his antipathy and blame up close where it would be undeniable and real.

It wasn't supposed to be like this! They had agreed to a harmless fling. Not something that would torture her to the depths of her soul forever.

The little she had read on relationships after divorce claimed they were often very intense and sexual and also that they stung like hell when they ended. She might have believed this was nothing more than a textbook case of rebound melancholy, but the way she felt went beyond the emotions that were forming a bleak aura around her. She was exhausted. Anemic, maybe. Her stomach wasn't quite right, either.

She had tried to dismiss it as stress-related, but yesterday, her divorce had been finalized. She had signed the papers and Neal was out of her life for good. She ought to be over the moon.

Maybe she needed to see a doctor. Given her travel and stress, she had probably picked up a virus. Maybe she'd been bitten by a deer tick when she'd been hiking through the woods in Tofino. Maybe a mosquito had given her some new exotic fever.

Ugh. She hated the idea of doctors so much. The mere thought of making an appointment gave her trauma flashbacks to all those invasive procedures trying to address her fertility issues. The last thing she wanted was to get poked or prodded or patronized again.

Wait.

She sat up so fast, her head swam. Her stomach twisted in hope and dread before she had fully done the math on her last cycle.

She dropped her head into her hands, trying to think through her ricocheting thoughts.

Her last one had been before Tofino. Two weeks before. She clearly remembered having a horrific backache when she went to see her lawyer. That date had been one year on the dot from when she had begun living away from Neal, marking the required year of separation.

It's not possible, she reminded herself. Doctors had said so. More than one.

But it was—technically—possible. The condom had broken.

No. Being pregnant right now, by Jasper, would be a disaster. He had been upset by the broken condom. He hadn't wanted the risk *before* she'd sent his plans off the rails. He wouldn't want a baby with her. No way.

Which was exactly the backhanded luck that convinced her to entertain the idea that maybe she could be pregnant.

Her heart began to flutter in an unfettered mix of excitement and trepidation.

Did she still have a test in the bathroom?

Her pulse slammed so hard that she was afraid to rise in case she fainted.

It's not possible. It's not possible.

After a few deep breaths, she rose to find out.

"Your divorce is final! That must be why you're glowing." Amelia swayed and patted Peyton's back while Vienna set out the clothes and teething toys she had bought for her niece in Germany.

Vienna didn't confess what was really lighting her up from the inside. The baby's father deserved to be the first to know—even if he was liable to be furious.

It didn't matter how he reacted, she assured herself. She was absolutely prepared to raise the baby alone. She was only telling him because their close alignment through family meant he would be aware of her baby and she didn't want him blindsided by any surprises in the future.

Of course, she might have dragged her feet a little if Amelia hadn't mentioned that Jasper was leaving for Santiago within the week.

"Oh? Do you have commitments with him before he leaves? I was thinking to finally take you up on a visit this weekend," Vienna had said, as if it was unrelated. "I want to hear all about Bora Bora and see my favorite niece."

"Bora Bora was all the *S*'s. Sun, sand, swim, sleep. Maybe that other *S* that goes along with a honeymoon." She winked through the camera. "I'll invite Jasper to come for dinner while you're here." Amelia's voice had dipped with curiosity. "I'm sure he'd like to say hello."

"If he's not too busy. I'd love to see him again." Vienna had fought to keep her voice at exactly the right balance of friendly without betraying anything more. *She* hadn't said anything more to Hunter and Amelia about her intimate relationship than her first report that Neal had misconstrued what he'd seen when he found them there together.

Neither had Jasper, apparently, because Amelia had only mentioned him in passing when Vienna arrived last night, saying he was very busy finalizing some things before his trip, but had agreed to come to dinner Saturday night.

Vienna had barely slept. Now she was on pins and needles, struggling to appear nonchalant while sneaking glances at the clock.

Peyton let out a robust burp.

"Is that how you thank Auntie when she's spoiling you?" Amelia wiped the chin of her grinning baby. "Give Auntie a proper hug." She tipped the baby into Vienna's lap, handing her the spit-up towel as well. "Just in case."

"Oh, sugarplum." Vienna hugged the warm little midge into her chest, enjoying the sensation of her toes digging into her thighs and not minding the pull of her hair in a tight fist.

It struck her that soon she would have her own small and mighty love machine to give her gooey kisses and wobbly bounces on her lap.

The specialist she'd seen had confirmed her pregnancy and assured her there was no reason to fear pregnancy loss. Not any more than the average first-time pregnancy, but after so many disappointments in her journey to getting pregnant, Vienna couldn't help worrying that this miracle wouldn't stick.

Those misgivings were cast away in a sudden rush of anticipation, however, when she wondered if her baby would look like her cousin Peyton. How magical!

Her eyes welled with such joy that Amelia might have noticed, but the doorbell rang.

"That's Jasper." Amelia slipped away to let him in.

Vienna hugged Peyton, trying to get hold of herself, but fresh nerves attacked. She was dying to see him, yet filled with trepidation. How would he react to her, let alone her news?

She heard them exchange a few words at the door. The timbre of his voice seemed to resound in her own ears, sending trickles of excitement down her shoulders and spine.

Amelia led him into the living room and a painful flash of nervous excitement struck Vienna, stealing her breath.

"Hunter's in his office," Amelia was saying. "Still playing catch-up from while we were away. I'll go down and tell him it's time to be sociable."

"No hurry," Jasper said, but Amelia was already trotting down the stairs, leaving a weighted silence behind her. "Vienna," Jasper said with a distant nod of greeting, staying by the windows instead of sitting down near her. "It's nice to see you again."

Not Vi. Vienna. Her mouth went dry.

Her whole being was reacting to him. He had a fresh haircut and had let his beard grow in, but wore it closely trimmed. His striped button shirt over suit trousers and polished shoes made her wonder if he'd come straight from the office, since these clothes seemed so much more formal than the ones she was used to seeing him wear.

Was it the clothes that made him appear so remote? He looked like the man she had felt so close to, the man she had longed to see again, but his flat mouth and lowered eyelids made him more inimical than ever. He struck her as even more guarded than he had been in the first moments when they had met.

His gaze flickered over her, his expression softening marginally when he looked at Peyton. That tiny, indulgent curl at the corner of his mouth gave her so much hope. It wrapped around her like a hug until his cool blue eyes lifted to hers again and sent a chill into her chest.

"It's good to see you, too." The pale platitudes sounded ridiculous, especially in her abraded voice. "I—" She looked over her shoulder, aware Amelia would be back with Hunter any second. "I need to tell you something."

He lifted inquiring brows.

She shifted forward and rose with Peyton still in her arms. As she took a few faltering steps toward him, she searched for the man who had shown her those brief moments of tenderness and understanding, but all she saw was enmity.

"This is hard to say." She glanced over her shoulder again. "I'm…"

Amelia and Hunter's voices were coming up the spiral staircase. The desire to put this off nearly overwhelmed her, but this was why she was here. To tell him. She needed him to know.

"I'm pregnant," she whispered.

"You're…" His brows flew upward and he rocked back on his heels, then held himself so still it was as if he had hardened to stone. Only the flare of his nostrils told her he was still breathing. "How? And why are you telling me? Are you saying *I'm*—" He jabbed the knife of his fingertips against his chest, then dropped his hand, cutting off his words as Amelia and Hunter appeared.

The other couple halted, sensing the wall of tension they'd walked into.

Vienna didn't know what to do except to look at Peyton. She was blissfully ignorant of these undercurrents. All she wanted to do was bounce and chew her own fist.

Vienna felt Jasper's outraged glare radiating against her cheek, though, and the bounce of her brother's attention striking her then Jasper and coming back to her.

"Jasper," Hunter said in a tone that held a bevel of warning. "You're also working on the weekend?"

"I was," Jasper said, shaking Hunter's hand in greeting.

"What can I get you to drink?" Hunter moved to the bar.

"It's so funny to me that you two already know each other," Amelia said, taking Peyton when the baby reached for her, but dividing her attention between Vienna and Jasper. "It's a dream come true for me to have you both here. Do you know that? Even when Jasper was missing, I would promise myself that one day he would join my new family for dinner and here we are." She beamed a huge, emotive smile at the pair of them.

"We can't stay," Jasper said flatly.

Amelia's face fell. "What? Jasper!"

"Jasper," Vienna urged softly.

"Vienna and I have things to talk about," Jasper said.

"What things?" Amelia demanded.

"Use my office." Hunter waved toward the stairs.

"No. We'll go to my place. Sorry, Melia." Jasper tried to kiss her cheek, but Amelia brushed him off.

"I made Mom's meatloaf. You *asked* me to," she said with annoyance.

"Good thing it freezes," he muttered. "Let's go." He jerked his head at Vienna.

"I'll have some later," Vienna promised. If she survived.

She veered her gaze from Amelia's shocked expression to her brother's grim, suspicious one before she followed Jasper out the door.

"We could have talked there," Vienna said beside him as Jasper drove toward his penthouse. "What are they going to think?"

"Who the hell cares what anyone thinks?"

She gasped as if he'd struck her. "That's really unfair, Jasper. I've never had the luxury of not caring what anyone thought about me."

"I guess you're right because I *thought* you couldn't get pregnant." He was still in shock. Feeling tricked. Behind that frontline anger was a closet loaded with emotions he had sealed a long time ago. The ones he was trying to keep at bay while he absorbed this news.

"I didn't lie to you! For heaven's sake, Neal—"
She cut herself off, covering her eyes in anguish.

He swore silently. He knew what she was
referring to. The way Neal had aired that particular detail about their marriage had been inordinately cruel, especially when Jasper had
witnessed how devastated Vienna had been
over her inability to conceive. He knew the
lengths she'd gone to when it came to trying
for a baby.

He was searching for the right words to apologize when she cried, "Would you *slow down*?"
She clasped the handle above the door.

He grappled himself under control, easing
up on the accelerator, but he took the shortcut
with the illegal left turn so he arrived at his
building sooner.

He parked and would have come around to
her door, but she flung hers open and threw
herself from the car, marching wordlessly
across the underground parking lot toward the
elevator.

She looked really good. That was what he'd
been thinking since seeing her on his sister's
sofa, hair loose, minimal makeup, smiling
warmly at the baby. Now he took note of the
way her blue jeans cupped her ass. He'd already admired the way her bohemian-style top

hugged her breasts. On first look, he'd taken it as a comfortable shirt for the changeable temperatures of an early fall day, but now he saw how its loose drape down to her hips made it a subtle and trendy maternity blouse.

How was he supposed to process this?

For the last month, he'd immersed himself in work, finalizing his takeover of REM-Ex while pushing for the investigation that was needed into Saqui's death. Did he blame Vienna for the fact that Orlin had sailed off into the horizon without facing the consequences for his crimes? Not exactly. Neal had pulled a fast one and was the one who had exposed Jasper, not Vienna. Despite a last-minute scramble for a new plan, Jasper was still able to make headway on cleaning up REM-Ex. Now that he had full access to his finances, he had also ensured Saqui's family was as comfortable as possible.

What he did resent was how persistently Vienna stayed on his mind. She chased him into his sleepless nights and her name was attached to any headline about him. The trolls and bots had figured out they were a sure-fire combo when it came to clicks.

Even his sister insisted on dropping her name into his consciousness.

Vienna's home from Germany.

Vienna's arranging us tickets to an art show.
Vienna's divorce is final.

Vienna's coming to visit this weekend. Would
you like to come for dinner?

He had agreed because it would be rude not
to. To get it over with. Between him and Vienna, they had managed to convince Hunter
and Amelia, and the world at large, that they
had platonically shared a house for a couple of
nights. Nothing untoward had happened.

Surely they could uphold that ruse for the
duration of one meal? He was leaving for Santiago within the week, so they wouldn't cross
paths again for a long while.

He had hoped this meeting would prove to
himself that whatever had gripped them in Tofino had been a mirage. He should have known
he was kidding himself when a twitchy restless-
ness had gripped him as he counted down the
hours to seeing her. When he had walked into
his sister's home, he'd felt Vienna's presence so
clearly it was as if he'd scented her. Every part
of him had reawakened in a way he hadn't felt
since the day he'd met her.

Even as an expanding force had risen in him,
he'd noticed she was wide-eyed with apprehension. She was bracing herself to face him, fearful of whatever he might say or do.

He'd done nothing. Or rather, he had tried to be as neutral as possible, but as his sister walked away and Vienna approached him, his abdomen had tightened with tension that had its roots in memory. In lust.

Nothing had prepared him for the blow she had delivered, though.

"This is lovely," she murmured as the elevator let them into his foyer.

It was an older building, but the endless views of Vancouver Harbor and Stanley Park had sold him the minute he'd walked in.

She spared a moment to admire the view, then froze as she saw what hung over the gas fireplace.

"Why did you frame it?" She walked across to the sketch she'd made of Peyton, now matted and framed behind a pane of glass.

"I like it." It felt telling that he'd gone to so much trouble, but he did like it and it was his niece. "What was I supposed to do? Tack it to the fridge with magnets? Do you want anything?" He went to the sideboard where he poured himself a whisky, neat.

"I didn't bring my purse or phone," she realized with a look at her empty hands. "But no. Thank you. I can't drink." She pointed at her middle, then folded her arms. "And yes, you are the father." Her voice shook. "Why else would I tell you?"

He could think of a few hundred million reasons. It was astonishing how many women had begun throwing themselves at him now that he was revealed to be one of Canada's wealthiest bachelors.

"You were just hobnobbing around Europe. It's none of my business if you were with anyone, but it does create other possibilities where your pregnancy is concerned."

"Really?" she choked. "Okay. Unlike perhaps *you,* I haven't been with anyone else." A white ring appeared around her lips. Her cheeks went taut. "And it's none of my business if you have slept around," she continued facetiously. "Obviously. But it does create the possibility that you have other pregnancies out there. Do you?"

He supposed he deserved to have his words thrown back at him like that. They still rankled.

"I do not," he said flatly. He couldn't seem to forget about *her.* He took a deep gulp of the fiery alcohol. "Tell me how it happened."

She coughed out another humorless laugh.

The condom had split. He remembered. Vividly.

And this was exactly the situation—another unplanned pregnancy—that had risen in his mind like a cold specter when it had. She had reminded him she couldn't get pregnant and he'd dismissed the whole thing from his mind, not wanting to wade through any of those old, conflicted emotions.

He held a threatening onslaught of feelings at bay now, watching as she rubbed her arms and paced a few steps to look out the windows again.

"The specialist couldn't explain why it happened with you and not with Neal," she said in a low, troubled voice. "Maybe the *lack* of stress? Once I was separated from him, I began eating better and sleeping better. I was happier. Or at least less unhappy. The doctor said that might have given my body a chance to level out, hormone-wise. Heal. She pointed out that the world is full of babies conceived after the mother was told she was sterile and decided to quit trying. Nature is mysterious. Sometimes it's a matter of taking the pressure off, she said. And different couples have different chemistry." Her cheeks went pink.

Yeah, they had a different level of chemistry all right. He could feel the pull of it even as he resisted fully accepting this news. It wasn't that he didn't want the baby. More like he didn't want to want it then discover she didn't.

"There's no real explanation for why I got

pregnant, but I definitely am. It's definitely yours."

"Okay. And?" His ears were ringing, and he was straining so hard to hear what she hadn't yet said. He didn't want to ask in case the answer wasn't what he wanted to hear.

What *did* he want to hear?

The tendons in her neck flexed and she seemed to lose more color. She blinked fast and seemed to pull a cloak of dignity around her, standing taller as she did.

"I realize this isn't something you asked for." Her voice thickened and her eyes grew brighter. "I'm informing you because you have a right to know."

Know what? *Breathe*, he reminded himself, barely able to hear her voice through the rushing in his ears.

"I'm not trying to obligate you. I have all the resources I need to raise it alone," she continued.

"You're having it." He felt numb. As though he stood outside his body.

"Yes! Oh my God, yes. How could you even question that when you know how much I want a baby!" Her eyes were wet, her voice soaked in raw emotion. "I want this baby *so much*."

He knew he was still holding his drink in

front of his lips, but his whole body was paralyzed. He hadn't realized how badly he had needed to hear those words. Hadn't realized how profoundly they would affect him. A wrench of emotion accosted him, crashing past the wall he'd reflexively erected because this was too big.

This was real now. He was becoming a father. *This* was the news that really took his feet out from under him. *Now* his life was fundamentally altered.

"I was hoping you would be happy." She dashed at her cheeks. "Or at least...not angry. I can't help that I cause so much trouble for you, Jasper. I don't mean to. I *swear*. That's why I'll raise it alone. You won't be involved at all. In fact, if you don't want to tell anyone you're the father, that's okay. I understa—"

"Like hell, Vi. If you're having this baby, then *we* are having a baby. This time, I'm one hundred percent involved."

CHAPTER NINE

"W-WHAT?" HER LIPS went numb. Her equilibrium wobbled from a tentative joy—that he seemed to want the baby—to deep confusion. "What do you mean, 'this time'?" Her tender stomach curdled.

Agony flexed across his expression and a muscle pulsed in his jaw.

"Oh my God." Realization struck with such a deep spear of jealousy she felt impaled by it. "Do you already have a child?" Even as her mind tried to fold that news into her current reality, she experienced a pang of anguish on his behalf, thinking he'd been shut out of his child's life in some way.

Neither reaction made sense because he wasn't hers to feel possessive or compassionate toward.

It was hitting her, however, that they were co-parents. The moment she had found out, she had wanted to tell him. She hadn't known how he would react. In her heart of hearts, she had hoped he would be the one person who might share her exuberant joy, but she'd also been prepared for a flat rejection.

She definitely hadn't begun to process how much of a role he would play in her child's life, not beyond offering him a choice as to whether he wanted to be involved. It had never once occurred to her that he might already have a child.

"No," he muttered, draining his glass and setting it aside. "That other pregnancy was terminated."

"When?" she blurted, then, "I mean, I'd like to know what happened if you're willing to tell me. Obviously it's affecting how you're reacting to this baby." She lowered herself onto the sofa, dazed by this news and the charged emotions radiating off him.

"It is." He acknowledged tightly. "It happened right after we lost Mom." He took another sip, his gaze focused on the past. "Dad and Amelia were wrecked. My entire future had gone gray. My girlfriend and I had been using condoms, but—"

"That's why you were so upset that day," she realized. That was why he had shut down and shut her out even before Neal had turned up.

"We took one stupid chance," he muttered. "I swore I'd never be so careless again. I was going to say to you that day that I would get you one of those pills if you wanted. But you said you couldn't get pregnant and I knew how much that upset you. I couldn't bring myself to say anything more about it." He ran his hand down his face. "How the hell am I this lucky?"

His tone suggested he didn't feel very lucky at all. That hurt. She felt like she'd won the lottery. She had!

"Do you resent her for what she decided to do?" she asked carefully.

"No. I genuinely don't. Her body, her choice. I support that all the way. She was seventeen, same as me. I sure as hell didn't know how I would have shouldered even more responsibility at that time, so I completely understand how overwhelmed she felt." He squeezed the back of his neck. "There was a part of me that was relieved it wasn't my decision to make. I'll admit that. Maybe, if things had been different, we would have gone on to marry and have a family at a better time, when we were both equipped to handle it."

"You were in love with her." Long tentacles of jealousy lashed and stuck to her skin, worming their stinging chemicals deep into her organs, making her heart writhe in agony.

"As much as the average teenager could be." He shoved his hands into his pockets. "Our feelings might have matured as we matured ourselves, but we didn't get a chance to find out. She went to stay with her aunt. I thought—" He swore and turned his face away so she couldn't read what was in it. "She sent her aunt to tell me she'd decided to terminate. Maybe she thought I would be angry or blame her. That's always bothered me, that she felt she couldn't tell me herself. It makes me feel like I failed her in some way. But I think her aunt wanted to do it, to get her own point across."

"Which was?" Cold fingers trailed down her spine, raising goose bumps of dread all over her back and shoulders.

His flinty expression became conflicted and grim, revealing how much the experience continued to ravage him.

"She said Annalise had realized she would have better prospects in the future. She could do better, so she didn't want to tie herself to me." He finally looked at her, gaze flat, expression stony, but she knew how much those sorts of words hurt. She knew all too well.

"That's really awful, Jasper. You didn't deserve that." Especially not when he was actually a very caring and conscientious and generous person.

"It *was* awful." He blue gaze narrowed to pierce into her.

"I wasn't trying to shut you out!" she insisted. "I'm still in shock that this has even happened. I wanted you to know because it felt like the right thing to do, but I had no idea how you would react. Given how I caused things to go sideways with your plans for REM-Ex, I couldn't expect anything from you."

She had only hoped, really hoped, that he would welcome this news the way she did. Maybe she had hoped for a welcome of another kind, too, for her, but that was definitely not something she had expected.

"*I* expect things from *myself*," he asserted. "Of course I'm obligated to my child, exactly as much as you are. I'm obligated to the woman who carries my baby. You are both my responsibility, Vienna. Starting now. Your divorce is final, right?"

"Yes. But no." She held up a finger that trembled, her mind hung up on that dreadful word: *obligated*. "My divorce is final, yes, but it took me *years* to make that happen. I fought really hard to get to this point where I make my own choices. I won't give that up for anyone."

"I'm not 'anyone.' I'm the father of your baby. And you should go have a quick chat with Amelia because, guess what? Babies run your life for roughly twenty years."

"I know that!" She was prepared to make *those* sacrifices. "I'm not saying you can't be involved, Jasper." She pushed the heels of her hands into her eyes. "But you can't sweep in here and tell me how it's going to be the second I tell you I'm pregnant. I haven't had time to *think*."

"What is there to think about? This isn't a case where more information changes the decision. You want the baby. I want the baby. It's basic anthropology that we stick together and do everything we can to give our child their best start."

"How? What are you suggesting? A loveless marriage? Been there, done that and no. I can't, Jasper. I *can't*. And you can't make me believe it's what you would want, either. Not after what you just said." Her voice cracked and she had to look away.

Was he still in love with Annalise? A little? That thought ate clean through her soul.

His hands were knotted into fists in his pockets, his jaw hard as ironwood.

"Your marriage was absent of more than love. From everything you told me, it lacked basic respect. We have that much."

"Do we?" she asked wildly. "You just accused me of sleeping around and trying to pawn someone else's baby off onto you."

He sighed and pinched the bridge of his nose.

"This caught me off guard," he said tightly. "Frankly, I have trust issues after the people who hired me killed my friend and tried to frame me for it. That's not on you, though, so I apologize for what I said."

Oh, he absolutely destroyed her when he was fair and recognized his own missteps. She buried her face in her hands again, trying to think of a reason to keep her distance from him.

"We both want this baby, Vi."

"That doesn't mean we'll work as a couple."

"We work very well as a couple." His voice curled with dark irony. "Too well."

She scowled at him for playing dirty by reminding her. His low blow was a sensual pulse between her thighs. His heated gaze insisted she remember how they had conceived that baby, promising more of that pleasure. As much of it as she could stand.

Her throat grew hot.

"Marriage has worked out for Amelia and Hunter," he pointed out.

"Of course Hunter fell for Amelia," she scoffed. "Who can help loving her? She's perfect." *I'm not.* That was the sharp pang that struck deep in her heart. She wanted to be loved. She really did.

"It's true I don't possess my sister's capacity for affection and warmth. I've always preferred to live alone, but I'm not walking away from my child. We owe our baby an honest effort at raising it together. Did you really tell me expecting I wouldn't want anything to do with you or the baby?" She thought there was a ring of injury beneath his disbelief. "Then why tell me at all?"

Her chest tightened as he forced her to confront her true motive in coming here. She looked to the ceiling, acknowledging she could have waited months to tell him. She could have lied for years, claiming to anyone who asked that the father was someone in Europe or an IVF donor.

The real reason she had wanted to tell him was because she had wanted an excuse to see him. To see.

She had wanted to see if he still wanted her.

Maybe he did, sexually, but what he really wanted was the baby. *Not* her.

Even so, that was alluring to her. She didn't want to do this alone if she didn't have to.

"I do want you involved," she said tentatively. "I just don't know how much."

"Well, I'm telling you I'm all in, one thousand percent."

"Please think about what you're saying, Jasper. You don't know what my life is really like." She rose to pace with agitation. "You've had a taste of the Waverly drama. We're very messy." She was. "Ask your sister how she likes it." She flicked her hand toward his phone.

"Is that what has you worried? That I'm afraid the press will say something ugly about me?"

"I promise you they will," she said with the agony of experience.

"I genuinely don't care. This baby has become my highest priority."

"Just like that?" She shook her head and flung out a hand. "You only found out about it twenty minutes ago."

"How long did it take for you?" he challenged, gaze clashing into hers.

Not even that long. In fact, she was already distressed that the press might denigrate their baby because they weren't married.

"Things have happened so fast. Can we take

a beat?" she pleaded. "There's actually a three-month rule—guideline, I guess—where you keep your pregnancy private in case…" She didn't even want to say it.

"Is that a concern? How are you feeling?" He came to stand in front of her, holding out one hand as if she might feel faint and he would have to catch her. "I should have asked already."

"Everything is fine." She laughed with bemusement at that hand, still offered for her to grasp, but there was a bleak fear behind her shaky smile that she couldn't completely disguise.

"What aren't you telling me?" He frowned.

"Nothing. I swear. It's me. The doctor said everything is normal." She absently rubbed at the cobalt blue polish staining her cuticle. "But I'm very aware that my body didn't cooperate with getting pregnant. I'm afraid to get too attached in case it lets me down again. I'm not being rational, I know that." She lifted her gaze, embarrassed at her irrational fears.

"Your caution is understandable. No part of this belongs online unless you choose to share it. If you want to keep this between us for now, I support that." He nodded. "What about physically? How do you feel?"

Her heart gave another swerve as he accepted her wishes without batting an eye.

"I feel okay." Her mouth didn't feel quite steady as she smiled wryly. "Normal for early pregnancy, I guess. I'm nauseous and tired. Some foods taste funny. Nothing I can't handle."

"Good." He nodded again, more thoughtful. "I don't mind waiting to announce things, and we can even keep this from family for now if that's what you prefer, but I want to operate on the assumption we'll be welcoming this baby together in…?"

"May," she provided, all of her beginning to tremble. This felt really monumental. She wasn't prepared for it.

"I was born in May." His harsh features eased into bemusement.

"Taurus. Stubborn."

"So I've been told. I refuse to believe it."

"Shocking."

They shared a faint moment of amusement, one that almost gave her a ray of optimism that they could at least go back to the companionable friendship they'd shared in Tofino.

"We'll go through this pregnancy together so anything that happens, happens to *us*. You won't have to face it alone," he said somberly.

Was he trying to make her cry?

"I think that's naive on your part, since it's *all* happening to me," she joked, but she understood what he was saying and she was deeply touched.

"I'm as invested in this baby as you are," he said, spelling it out.

She swallowed, blinking her hot eyes. His words were beyond heartening, especially given how alone she had felt through all her past disappointments.

"Besides, we should take advantage of this time to get to know each other before the baby changes everything."

"You want to live together? Here?" She glanced around the penthouse with fresh eyes, thinking she might like that, especially with Amelia and Hunter so close by.

"Eventually here. Initially, in Santiago."

"Wait. What?"

"Are you sure about this, Vi?" Hunter leaned in the doorway of the guest bedroom that she used when she visited him here in Vancouver. "Fealty to my wife demands I believe Jasper is as solid a person as was ever built, but you just got out of a rough marriage. You spent a couple of days with him a month ago and you're prepared to follow him to Santiago? How well do you know him?"

"That's kind of the point." She smiled blithely, refusing to show any of her misgivings.

They had come back for dinner last night and announced that Vienna would be accompany Jasper to Santiago; there had been no mention of the baby. Hunter and Amelia were surprised, but Amelia had recovered quickly, saying how thrilled she was that they were getting together.

"We might have got to know each other better in Tofino if we'd had the chance," Vienna told Hunter. "Since Jasper has to be in Santiago for a time, and I have flexibility, it makes sense for me to go with him. I'm looking forward to getting away from the attention here and checking out the art scene there. If things aren't working out, I'll come home."

Please let it work out. She folded her top and smoothed it down her front, wondering what "work out" would look like. Love. That's what. She couldn't settle for anything less. Not again, but she couldn't shake her nagging fear that she wasn't the sort of person anyone loved.

"Why was he so upset last night when you two left?" Hunter asked.

"I told you." She hated lying to him, but this was at least a partial truth. Jasper *had* been concerned when she had told him about her conversation in Germany. "When I was at the wedding, I mentioned to Micah and Remy that something fishy was going on with REM-Ex. I thought it was simple good manners to warn them if they happened to be invested there. Jasper pointed out that it doesn't look good on him if I started a whisper campaign while he was acquiring shares."

"Remy would never reveal his source."

"I don't think Micah will, either. Neither of them had shares anyway. Micah sold his ages ago."

"How was the wedding?" Hunter asked with mild interest.

"Beautiful." She couldn't help smiling as she remembered it. "Quinn and Micah seem very happy."

"And Eden?" A shadow of concern flickered across Hunter's expression.

"Also very happy." She set her blouse into the suitcase. "I'll apologize one last time for setting you up with her and promise *not* to pursue a career in matchmaking."

"Good thing. I'm pretty sure you'd starve," he teased. "Do you want me to carry that down?" He nodded at her suitcase as she closed it.

"Thanks. Are you really worried about my

going to Chile with Jasper?" She chewed the corner of her lip.

"Not worried exactly." He hefted the case. "Disappointed. I prefer having you close by. I'll miss you if you're so far away."

"Toronto is 'close'?"

"Five hours is better than sixteen. At least I go to Toronto every few months."

"I like this sentimental softie you're turning into." She lightly poked his chest.

He responded by giving her hair a tug. "I want you to be happy, Vi. You're sure that this will do that for you?"

She wasn't, but… "There's only one way to find out."

He cocked his head in acceptance of her logic and took her case down to Jasper's car.

CHAPTER TEN

JASPER HAD PLANNED to fly commercial, but with Vienna coming along, he chartered a private jet and hired a maternity nurse to travel with them, one who would stay to provide prenatal care until Vienna found a doctor in Santiago.

The charter allowed them to fly earlier, which meant they would have a few days to get settled before he went into the office every day. He wanted to ensure Vienna was comfortable.

He was still trying to wrap his head around becoming a father. He'd always been of two minds on the idea. Growing up, he had assumed he would create a life like the one he had known—a stable, loving family with a wife and children.

Then he'd lost his mother, which had given him a front-row seat on his father's grief, and had been judged not worthy of being a husband and father. That had messed with his ability to see himself in the role. That was why he'd been so careful in the ensuing years, refusing to put himself in the position of a surprise pregnancy again.

Despite that, he wasn't the least bit conflicted on whether he wanted *this* baby. A persistent ache of impatience sat behind his sternum. He wanted to hold their baby *now*. Vienna's concerns were sobering, making him all the more protective and urgent to get through the pregnancy so he could be hands-on with looking after their baby. At that point, it really would be a team effort on ensuring their child thrived.

Were they a team? He didn't do group activities, and when he did, he led.

Pressing her to come with him, to try to form a family, was in their child's best interest. He stood by that. But he did have certain misgivings about their relationship. They came from very different worlds and all they really shared was a baby.

And the heat with which they'd conceived it.

He was trying not to dwell on that, even though it was definitely a factor in why he'd pushed her to come with him. Could she even have sex? He hadn't yet asked. He'd been focused on the immediate business of yanking her firmly back into his life while trying not to hold a grudge over what had happened with REM-Ex.

"Can I ask you something?" Vienna asked quietly. She dragged her eyes from where the nurse was watching a movie, her ears covered by noise-canceling headphones.

"Yes?" He lifted inquiring brows.

"Why—" She seemed briefly perplexed and a little self-deprecating. "I'm wondering how rich you are and why you didn't tell me? Which I know is rude, but I had the impression in Tofino that REM-Ex had much deeper pockets than you did. I was surprised when I heard you had bought them."

"I'm rich enough that we'll need a robust prenup if we decide to marry." It circled back to that moment in the grocery store parking lot and a burning need to prove himself to a woman who had forgotten him the moment she turned her car back onto the street.

"You're insulted. I shouldn't have asked." She wrinkled her nose.

"I'm offended that I was ever judged on what I have or didn't have. Orlin Caulfield made the same mistake, thinking I wasn't his equal."

"You're not."

He snapped a look at her.

"You're far more than he could ever hope to be, whether you own REM-Ex or not."

Those eyes of hers could drown him if he wasn't careful.

"What's going to happen to him?" she asked. "Is it dangerous for us to be in Santiago? I heard you talking to someone about upping security to include me."

"That's an abundance of caution. I asked a firm to shadow us for a few weeks, to confirm there's nothing to worry about. I wouldn't have brought you if I thought it was dangerous for you. No." He shook his head. "There was a rash of firings and resignations when I took over. The guilty ran for cover, but they're hoping to get away with their crimes, not come back on me for exposing them. Mostly my takeover has been greeted with enthusiasm because I'm cleaning house."

"And the investigation into Saqui's death?"

"I have an email that shows Orlin Caulfield ordered the landslide. I don't know if I'll ever find the person who set off the charge, but Orlin is the one behind all of this. The investigation has moved into calculating a settlement number for the Chilean authorities for the environmental damages, which I support. The REM-Ex lawyers are already filing a list of charges against Orlin for misrepresentation and other corruptions. There are liens on his Canadian assets pending the outcome, so he's definitely enjoying a taste of what he served me. He's unable to access his money and is stuck on his boat with few ports of call where he won't be arrested and extradited."

"Are you satisfied with that?"

"For now." He would never be satisfied. Not until Orlin was rotting behind bars.

"What I mean is, I don't want it between us that I ruined your plan to have him arrested."

"It's not."

Her mouth quirked to a skeptical angle as she searched his gaze.

They really did have a distance to go before they trusted one another. Fine. He went with brutal honesty.

"For Saqui's sake, I can't rest until Orlin is in jail, but it's not productive for me to keep it between us, so I'm doing my best to let it go," he said.

She flinched and looked away, nodding jerkily. "At least I know where I stand."

Sensitive, he remembered with a pinch of chagrin. She felt everything twice as hard as most people.

Grudges had always been his fuel, though.

He didn't know how to operate without feeling that burn of rancor inside him.

What more did he need, though? What did he want to prove? To whom? Vienna?

You're far more than he could ever hope to be.

"I'm going to lie down in the stateroom," she said, unbuckling. Avoiding his gaze.

It was barely eight o'clock Vancouver time, but he nodded and watched her go.

They had left the drizzle of autumn in Vancouver for early spring in Chile. Snow on the Andes formed a backdrop to a fascinating city of contrasts. The green spaces had yet to green up, but thick vines and tall palms grew in abundance between old-world stone buildings and glass skyscrapers. The bright, sunny sky cast deep shadows into narrow streets where elderly women ran flower shops brimming with fragrant blossoms.

All of these things managed to distract Vienna from her concern that she and Jasper didn't really stand a chance, not if he continued to resent her.

He seemed to be genuinely trying to smooth things over, though.

After they checked into their penthouse suite

in the hotel, they napped and freshened up from travel, then ambled through the downtown area to have lunch with a property agent.

The woman was excited by the idea of a generous commission and couldn't wait to get started.

"I was thinking to leave the house-hunting in your capable hands," Jasper said as they walked through a park on the way back to their hotel. "Would you feel comfortable if she took you around without me? The security detail would go with you."

"I don't mind doing it alone if you're too busy, but would you trust me?" They had talked with the agent about finding something they could call "home" at least part-time for the next several years—which felt very permanent when their relationship was still so delicate. Vienna was holding her breath, convinced any misstep on her part could wreck everything.

"Did you not agree with the direction I thought we should take?" He had told the agent they wanted several bedrooms so family could visit for extended periods, along with room for entertaining and accommodation for staff. He wanted grounds that offered a sense of privacy and a pool if possible. "In terms of style, I liked your place in Tofino."

"Hunter found that house."

"Yes, but we both liked it, so we have similar tastes. You'll have opinions about what might work as a studio, too."

That had been her contribution to the wish list, but, "What if I reject something you might think is perfect?"

"If you don't like it, how could I see it as perfect?"

She halted in the middle of the wide path. For a second, she could only stare at him.

"What?" His brows came together over the mirrored lenses of his sunglasses.

She started to dismiss her astonishment, then admitted with a flex of shame in her brow, "It still surprises me when you're so considerate. I'm not used to it."

His sighed out a subdued rumble of discontent and they continued walking.

"We both bring baggage into this relationship," he said with deliberate patience. "We're going to leave it out sometimes and the other one will trip over it. But I'd rather not be compared to your ex if you can help it."

"I don't. Believe me, there is no comparison on that front," she said with a husk of humorless laughter because it was so true. Jasper could tell her right now that he didn't think they would work after all and he would be miles ahead of Neal on the honesty and consideration scale. "Neal wasn't the only one who really didn't give a damn about what I wanted or needed, though."

She hated admitting that. There was always a lingering fear that maybe the way she'd been treated was her own fault because she genuinely didn't measure up. Maybe it was only a matter of time before Jasper saw it, too.

"Your stepmother?" he asked. "I thought she was... I don't know. A narcissist?"

"She was. And a sex addict, I think? She definitely had a troubling relationship with alcohol and drugs."

"Why did your father stay married to her?"

"I don't know. But his reason doesn't matter, only that he did. And the fact he took her side makes him just as bad as she was, in my opinion." She paused as they came up to the lip of a giant fountain filled with shiny coins. "It makes him worse, I think, because he should have protected me from her, but he sided with her instead."

"Where was Hunter all this time?"

"Being a child, too!" She would never hear a word against him. He ought to get used to that. "Hunter was dealing with the same thing I was—being belittled and humiliated at any sort of gathering because she refused to wear underwear and loved to dance on tables." Among thousands of other things. "Hunter did what he could, standing up for me and talking to Dad, but he started working at Wave-Com in high school. The board pressured him to rein her in, as if it was up to him to be responsible for two grown adults! I know he felt guilty, leaving me alone with them when he went to university, but it wasn't like I was in danger." Not physically, anyway.

"That's not the sort of father I intend to be," he said gravely.

"I know." She started walking again, offering a polite smile to a woman who walked by with her miniature schnauzer. "But they did leave me with horrible self-esteem issues." It was so lowering to admit that. She had grown up and moved past a lot of it, but that kind of baggage lingered and still ambushed her sometimes. "Everyone always asks me why I don't work at Wave-Com and the answer is that I asked Dad if I could, when I was fifteen. I wanted to job-shadow in the marketing department for a school assignment."

"Why would he refuse? Graphics. Art. That's right in your lane." He glanced at her again.

"Irina laughed so hard." Vienna could still hear the cruel ring of it. "She said I wasn't smart enough to work at the company. That I would only embarrass Dad by being there. Granted, my grades were very average, but—"

"It was a job-shadow. A *day*."

"He said no and I couldn't bring myself to ask again. Ever. I should have known better than to ask at the time. It didn't matter what I wanted to do, Irina would mock me for it. Puberty was absolute hell, when I was growing into my body. She always wanted to be the center of attention, even if that meant getting negative attention by insulting me in front of my friends or criticizing my sketches in an art competition. The online trolls loved what they saw as a feud between us, when it was really just her saying mean things about me. That's why I'm still such an easy target for them. She trained them."

"Where is she now?" Jasper asked in a falsely pleasant tone.

"Marrying Orlin Caulfield, if there's a god."

He barked out a laugh.

"The point is, she did a number on my belief that I can do anything right. It doesn't help that I'm human and actually do make mistakes. The marriage that was supposed to prove to my father that I was an asset to the company turned into a disaster. Then, when I filed for divorce and thought, *There, I'm putting that behind me and starting with a clean page...*"

They shared a wry look.

"I'm glad you told me this." He took her hand as they came out of the park and steered toward the pedestrian crossing to their hotel. "I'm going to guess she was jealous because you're actually very beautiful. I'm sure she felt threatened by that."

Vienna must have winced at that because he said, "Vienna," with a mix of gentle scold and astonishment. "Please tell me you know how beautiful you are."

"I know how to tick the boxes on what most people think is beautiful," she said helplessly as they moved into the portico of the hotel. "Blond streaks and shaped brows and..." She brushed at the stylish linen culottes she wore with a bralette and satin blazer. "Fooling people into thinking I'm beautiful isn't the same as being beautiful."

She released his hand to skip into the revolving door then crossed the lobby, trying to get away from that conversation, but Jasper brought it into the elevator with them.

He leaned on the wall, staring at her. "The

most beautiful woman I have ever seen was wearing my T-shirt and no makeup. She didn't even have her hair brushed. It was all piled on her head with a crunchie—"

"Scrunchie," she corrected, laughing, but also blushing. She remembered that morning all too well.

"She told me to stand still and wasn't even looking at me, which drove me *crazy*. So all I could do was look at her."

"I *was* looking at you! I was drawing you."

"And you looked so happy doing it that I wanted to stand there forever." He launched himself across the elevator and caged her against the opposite wall. "But it was so freaking erotic I couldn't handle it. And you *didn't even notice*."

"Buddy, I was drawing you." She tapped the middle of his chest. "Just because it was from the waist up doesn't mean I wasn't aware of what was going on below the edge of the page."

His hot gaze drifted to her mouth and he might have kissed her, but the bell pinged and the doors opened.

He straightened away and motioned to the German-speaking couple that the car was going up, not down. They were left alone again.

Vienna looked to him, expecting—hoping—

he would come back to her, but he was facing straight ahead now, his cheeks hollow.

"It was a good drawing," he said, as if the flirtatious lunge hadn't happened. "I kept the sketchbook. It's in Vancouver. I meant to give it to you."

"I have dozens of sketchbooks and I'm not afraid to buy more." It was true. Some women had a shoe fetish. Hers was an eternal search for exactly the right tooth on the right size of ivory paper, bound in a way that pleased her.

They entered their spacious suite. It was tastefully decorated in whites and blues and silver. The drapes were pulled back on the wall of windows, offering gorgeous views of Santiago and the mountains. Through a pair of double doors, the king-size bed still showed the wrinkles from their nap when they had arrived.

Would they use it for anything more than sleeping?

Vienna glanced again at Jasper, wondering how to open that conversation when that, too, was baggage she still carried.

He was looking at her.

"What?" she asked, glancing down at her jacket to see if she'd spilled something at lunch.

"I've been thinking about asking the nurse something."

The nurse had her own room on a lower floor. Aside from checking in daily and responding to texts, she was mostly free to do her own thing.

"But it just occurred to me that it doesn't matter if she says you're allowed to have sex. The question is whether you want to. I understand if you have reservations, given how delicate—"

"Jasper," Vienna cut in with absolute astonishment. "Did you seriously bring me all this way believing we might not have sex?" Her cheeks began to sting. "I mean, I presumed we would, but…" She cleared her throat. "I mean, I didn't come all this way *not* to have sex."

"No?" He sauntered toward her. More like stalked.

Her pulse began to race and her body screamed an enthusiastic *Yes*. The rest of her was searching his features for signs this was more than sex for him.

Which wasn't realistic. She knew it wasn't. In reality, they'd only spent a few days in each other's company, but he had filled her thoughts for the month they'd been apart. She was starting to feel as though she knew him well enough to know that deeper feelings were only a short stumble away—for her, anyway.

She really wanted to believe he was coming right along with her, though.

"Don't worry, Vi." He misread her expression and gathered her close, smoothing her hair behind her ear. "I can go slow and gentle." He ran his tongue over his teeth. "Previous performance notwithstanding."

"I don't know if you noticed, but I didn't submit any complaints. In fact, I left you five stars."

"Was that you? I wasn't sure if TofinoBabe was you or— Ouch." He caught the hand pinching his stomach and the corner of his mouth kicked up in a very sexy grin, one that had her catching her breath at how handsome he was. "I don't kiss and tell, but of *course* you get all the stars. There aren't enough stars for how great sex with you feels."

Just sex, then. She grabbed at the heart that was tipping forward into the abyss, but it remained right on the edge as she stared into the banked hunger of his eyes.

"We can take our time, you know. We have lots." His finger was still tracing her ear, making fine hairs stand up at the back of her neck. "Tell me what you need."

She opened her mouth, but words wouldn't form. He was barely touching her and she wanted to melt right into him.

She set her hand on his chest, unable to resist

trailing light fingers across the hard muscle of his pec, then finding the nipple that puckered beneath the crisp fabric.

His chest swelled and his head dipped, but his lips only went into her neck. At first, all she felt was his breath. A hot swirl against sensitized skin, then the lightest nuzzle of his lip.

She whimpered, knees softening.

His arms around her tightened. "I haven't even kissed you yet."

She knew. The effect he had on her was magnificent in its devastation. It was terrifying. A loss of self every time, but she succumbed all the same.

He was determined to conquer her in his own time, though. It was a small frustration when she wanted the heat and the blindness. She wanted to know he was as affected by her as she was by him, but he refused to be rushed. He slid his hands in slow circles all over her back and hips, brushing his lips in those kisses that made her hurt inside because they were so tender.

"Jasper," she whispered in a small plea.

"Let me learn," he chided, his voice just as soft while his hands skimmed the satin of her jacket, rubbing it against her skin. He released the button at her navel and pressed the lapels open.

"This has been driving me crazy," he growled, bracketing her waist with his palms and sliding his thumb along the scalloped band beneath her breasts. "Is this a bra? Are you wearing one under it? No," he answered himself as his thumbs climbed higher, discovering her nipples.

"Careful." She sucked in a breath. "They're sensitive."

He made a crooning noise and his touch gentled. His mouth skimmed her brow and the point of her cheek before his teeth caught her earlobe.

"Every night, I think about touching you again," he confessed. "I think about the stairs and our kiss in the woods when I wanted to have you against that tree. It wasn't enough. None of it. I wanted this. More time. More."

A strangled noise broke from her throat. Her hands were sliding over him, pulling his shirt from his trousers, seeking hot skin, but even though he groaned and his whole body flexed, he kept to the slow slide of his hands and the unhurried brush of his lips along her jaw toward her mouth.

With a noise of frustration, she cupped his head and caught at his lips with her own, pressing her tongue past the seam of his lips.

He grunted, but dragged his hands up to her hair and threaded his fingers into the length. The weight of his hands pulled her head back so her mouth was tilted up for his and he lifted away so he was fully in control, barely touching her with the teasing graze of his lips against hers.

"Kiss me," she demanded.

"I am," he assured her, pressing soft, soft kisses against her upper lip, then her chin, her throat. Sensual lips found their way down her breastbone before his teeth opened over the cup of her bra.

She didn't know how to process this many sensations, this much attention and care. She ran her fingers through his hair and shaped the base of his skull, sliding her touch beneath his collar before seeking the line where his shaved throat met the stubble of his thickening beard.

"You scare me," she admitted as he released the zip on her culottes and they started to slide off her hips.

He paused. "Stop?"

"No. Keep going. *Please* keep going." Her voice was jagged.

But leave me something. He was stealing every inch of her soul, one kiss and caress at a time.

"What scares you?" His mouth was on her collarbone, his clever fingers tracing the satin and lace of her underwear.

"How you make me feel…it's too much." But yet also not enough.

She couldn't bear the anticipation. While her flesh cried out for the caress of his, she yanked at his belt and opened his fly, then slid her hand inside his briefs. Velvet over steel met her questing touch. Hot, fierce arousal and a tender tip that made his breath hiss when she caressed him.

He yanked up his head to reveal the way lust had shattered his vision before he crushed her mouth with his. His arm around her held her tight as he rocked his mouth across hers while one fingertip quested beneath satin.

When he found the moisture, he spread it around, sliding his touch upward, parting her, lifting his head to watch desire diffuse her vision. His tongue licked flagrantly along her bottom lip while he caressed her in the most blatant ways.

"How close are you? Let me watch," he rasped. One finger invaded, two. The heel of his palm pressed against the knot of nerves at the top of her sex, making her shake. Making her rock her hips in craving.

She clung one arm around his neck. The other squeezed him in a fist while her hips lifted into his touch. She couldn't help herself. She *needed* this.

"Softly, softly," he whispered, but this was too profound to be soft. Her body clamped onto his intruding fingers and her hips rolled, trying to catch the wave that would take her to the top. That one…? That one? Oh, yes, *this* one.

With a tortured groan, she gave herself up to the rapture.

She's here. She's not going anywhere, he kept telling himself, trying to dull his greed, but the wolf in him was hungry, so damned hungry and horny and howling.

The clothes between them were an affront. He dealt with them while she was still limp on the bed, catching her breath.

Oh, he liked being responsible for that flush on her skin and the glassy haze in her eyes. When he stretched out atop her, the only thing that kept him lucid was her slight flinch as his arm brushed the side of her breast.

He had to be careful with her. He knew that. Not because her pregnancy was delicate, but because she was. She was sensitive, her heart easily bruised. She was so damned good at hiding it that he forgot at times, but she was an artist in her soul, feeling everything.

A ferocious rush of tenderness and a need to protect overcame over him, the kind that felt so juvenile he instinctually shied from letting it fully envelop him. He had to protect himself, too, right?

Yet, as her legs brushed his and her fingertips stroked his shoulder and neck and her abdomen quivered under the weight of his splayed hand, he knew she was already in possession of more of him than he was comfortable giving up.

He wanted to devour her. Fill himself up with her. But when he set his mouth on her trembling lips, he lingered, drawing out the kiss, taking his time to deepen it and slowing each of his caresses. He was putting off the moment when he would lose himself in her while stealing more of her, drinking in the way her arms curled around him.

He needed these signs that her defenses were utterly vanquished. It was the only way he could let down his own shields. He reveled in the way she opened her legs, inviting him, while her mouth pressed damp, desperate kisses across his chest. She set her teeth against his biceps and rolled her tongue across his nipple and her nails grazed his buttocks in helpless urging for him to press inside her.

Condom, he thought once. But they didn't need one.

He shifted her beneath him. She was more than ready. He slid deep in one thrust.

It felt too naked. Too profound. A harsh groan left him at the delicious, melted heat of her, but he was stripped to the very essence of his being. Elemental.

His arms shook when he braced himself over her, trying to physically hold himself apart, but she threw her head back, throat exposed, skin damp and glowing. His. All his.

He fought to keep it slow. He surged into her with careful power, luxuriating in the sheer perfection of her, enjoying the way she writhed beneath him and released throaty noises of anguished joy with each thrust.

This was what he had been craving in the weeks since they'd parted, this evidence that she was as powerless against this desire as he was.

And powerless he was. Despite taking it slow, despite his focus on driving her inexorably toward culmination, his grasp on control grew slippery and weak. Electrified tingles worked their way down his spine. It took everything he had to hold on and wait for her.

This gentle lovemaking should have resulted in a gentle release, but when she twisted beneath him, and her mouth opened in a silent scream, he felt the intensity of her climax in her convulsive squeezes.

Her pleasure triggered his. An orgasm crashed through him with cataclysmic force, brutal in its strength and unrelenting in its duration.

He was lost, utterly lost to her, but in those euphoric moments he didn't give a single damn.

CHAPTER ELEVEN

IT WAS AS good as she remembered. That was what Vienna was thinking after several days of near constant lovemaking. Sex with Jasper was actually better than she remembered because they were both getting to know each other's bodies, learning how to truly drive the other past their endurance of pleasure. This morning, she had joined him in the shower and blew his mind, leaving him sagged against the tiled wall, catching his breath and promising sensual retribution when he got home later.

She had never felt so confident in her sexuality. If this relationship failed and she walked away with a shattered heart, she still wouldn't regret being with him because he had given her a belief in her desirability.

Sex wasn't enough to build a future on, though. Was she being greedy or impatient to want a signal that he felt more for her?

She was ruminating on that, struggling to pay attention to the agent as she showed her yet another house, when her phone dinged with a text from him.

Saqui's parents are here, meeting lawyers. Dinner with them tonight?

Of course, she replied back.

Vienna wasn't sure what to expect from the dinner, but Jasper was withdrawn when he came back to the hotel to change and collect her. Usually their hello kiss turned into more, but he only pecked her cheek and asked how her day had gone.

"No luck today, but the agent said she's getting a better sense of what we're looking for. She'll have more to show me later in the week."

"Good." He was so distracted that it bordered on hurtful, but she was pretty sure his mood wasn't about her. This must be a difficult and emotional meeting for him.

She slipped on a scoop-necked blue dress and gathered her hair in a chignon, not talking until they were ready to leave.

"You look very nice," she told him as she made a tiny adjustment to his tiepin.

"So do you." He was still brisk, but he paused

to study her, then took her hand and wove their fingers together as they walked down to the waiting car.

Saqui's parents were already at the restaurant when they were shown to a table in an al fresco courtyard. An accordion player's notes floated on the soft air while strings of light gave it a soothing, magical atmosphere.

The Melillas were warm and welcoming, hugging Jasper and cupping his face while smiling widely. They were delighted he had brought his *novia* to meet them.

Vienna was still working on her Spanish, and thought that might mean bride or fiancée, but Jasper wasn't hiding that they were involved romantically. He touched her often through the meal, squeezing her hand or knee or setting his arm on her chairback and grazing her shoulder with his fingertips.

"Artista excepcional," he told them at one point and took out his phone, proceeding to show them her sketches of Peyton.

That prompted Saqui's mother to ask teasingly, *"Cuándo tendrás un bebé propio?"*

Vienna caught "when" and "baby." A hot blush of exposure rose in her throat, but Jasper took her hand and caressed her palm.

"That's something we would both welcome,

wouldn't we?" he said, looking at her with so much tenderness she blushed even harder.

She nodded shakily as he repeated the comment in Spanish and the other couple wished a big family for them.

When they said their goodbyes, Mrs. Melilla hugged her and said in Spanish, "It's good to see him happy."

Vienna wanted to believe he was, but he was very quiet on the way back to their hotel.

"That was really hard for you," she noted when they were in their room, changing into something more comfortable.

"It was," he agreed, yanking at his tie. "They don't blame me. They said so, but I feel so damned responsible anyway."

"What was Saqui like? Funny, like his dad?" Mr. Melilla had cracked her up a few times, leaning over with a silly aside.

"So funny. And smart. Unafraid. Grounded. I liked that about him a lot. He was ambitious, but he wasn't materialistic. He wanted a good job so he could support a wife and have a big family. Family was so important to him. If I could at least—"

He cut himself off, but she knew what he was going to say. If he could only put Orlin Caulfield behind bars, he might not feel so awful about moving forward with his own life.

"I'm not throwing that on you again," he clarified into the silence that had fallen between them. "I'm frustrated there isn't more I could do for them, to ease their loss."

And his own?

"I know," she murmured, recognizing his reticence with her for what it was: survivor guilt. If one little thing had been different, Saqui might have lived. "I'm really sorry you lost your friend." She moved closer and slid her arms around his waist. "He sounds like a really good person."

Jasper turned to stone as she touched him, but now he took a shaken breath.

"He was." His arms closed convulsively around her. "He really was."

They stood like that a long time.

Jasper had thought living with Vienna would be an adjustment, maybe even claustrophobic at times. Surprisingly, he liked the domestic routine they fell into, especially once they moved into their new home.

Vienna had found a stunning house situated at the foot of Manquehue Hill in the upscale Vitacura neighborhood. It was not unlike the

Tofino house in its terraced architecture. The tree-lined property and the hill rising behind the house gave the impression they were the only house for miles. Abundant windows looked to the lawn, the gazebo next to the pool, and views of the city lights in the distance.

Here in the primary bedroom, no expense had been spared. The palatial suite had its own sitting area, the dressing room where he currently stood, and a massive bathroom awash in luxurious touches. On its private terrace, there was an outdoor shower and a claw-foot tub open to the elements where Vienna liked to soak in fragrant bubbles.

Any of the other three bedrooms on this level would be perfect for a nursery, but when Jasper had glanced at her while touring the house, she had pointed to the room closest to where they slept. They were still keeping the pregnancy news quiet so decorators hadn't yet been hired, but he glanced in there every time he came upstairs, picturing it occupied.

On the main level, there was both a formal living room and a casual family room. The dining room table sat twelve, but they tended to eat on the terrace or on the breakfast patio off the long, narrow kitchen. It was full of stainless steel appliances, managing to be both functional and welcoming.

The bottom floor had a wine cellar, which was overkill for their needs, as was the cinema room with a bar. They were converting that into a guest suite with a kitchenette so family would be comfortable staying for long periods.

Finally, the home gym had already been emptied so Vienna could use it as a studio. Its high band of windows allowed natural light to pour in and its private courtyard with mature trees and flowerpots was the meditative atmosphere she liked to work alongside.

Thinking of her studio reminded him to take a closer look at his shirt. Rainbow-colored fingerprints occasionally showed up when he interrupted her work with a questing kiss.

He shifted while he finished buttoning his shirt so he could see her in the mirror where she was sleeping off their early morning lovemaking.

The sex only got more amazing, which obviously contributed to his satisfaction with their living together, but they had enough outside interests that their relationship wasn't all one note. He was still restructuring at REM-Ex, hiring and meeting with officials and implementing new procedures. She had reached out to some of her clients back in Canada, telling them about various artists she she had found here in Chile, continuing the curating work she'd been doing back home.

Vienna insisted art was a wise investment and had also begun a collection for him that had earned appropriate compliments when they had held a housewarming party last weekend.

That had been a game changer for Jasper. He still felt very middle-class, but given his ownership of an international mining firm, he felt obliged to entertain executives and dignitaries. Vienna had said the housewarming was a perfect excuse. He hadn't looked forward to it at all, but she had made all the arrangements and it had been a tremendous success. Everyone had raved about how *encantadora*—charming—his "wife" was.

He hadn't corrected anyone, but the more he thought about it, the more he wanted to call her that. His wife.

It was strange to feel so compelled when he had carried a resistance to the institution of marriage for so long. After witnessing his father's agony on losing his spouse, and suffering his own rejection, Jasper had avoided thoughts of marriage. He still felt enormous guilt that

Saqui couldn't carry on with life the way he was, but this would be for their child.

And Vienna, obviously. It was vitally important to him that she be looked after in the best possible way. Marriage to him would ensure she and their child had the absolute strongest foundation and rights to all he possessed.

It made sense and, armed with that rationale, he was impatient to close the deal, but she had made clear that she had certain reservations about planning for the future. She wanted to feel sure about the baby before she could feel secure in anything else. He was trying to respect that, but his mind drifted to buying a ring anyway.

Tomorrow. He was tied up today, but tomorrow he would shop for a ring. A day studying gemstones was pretty much his idea of Christmas and birthday combined so he was already looking forward to it.

"You're up early," she murmured, rolling over in the reflection of the bed behind him.

"Meetings with the Environment Superintendency today." He finished knotting his tie and centered it.

"What time?"

"All day. We're flying out to the site, but I'll be home at my regular time."

"Oh. I thought…" She sat up. "Well, that's important, obviously."

It was. He'd been trying to meet with this branch of government since he and Vienna had arrived six weeks ago. Until he had them on his side, his efforts to restart mining were dead in the water.

She looked crestfallen, though.

"What's wrong?" He turned.

"Nothing." She rearranged her features, obviously not realizing he'd seen her disappointment in the mirror. "I have my first scan today. I thought you wanted to come."

"That's tomorrow." How had he got that wrong? He reached for his phone and there it was in their shared calendar. His attendance was marked "optional," so he had accepted his own day being blocked for the other commitment, not reading this one closely enough.

He swore. "I'll see what I can do."

"I'm sure everything will be fine." She was doing that thing where she acted unbothered, sitting taller and manufacturing a pleasant smile. "I'll text you after."

"You're sure?" What if—No. He refused to borrow trouble.

"It will be fine," she insisted. "But I have a video chat with one of my clients before I leave for the clinic. I should get in the shower." She rose and slipped into the bathroom.

Vienna was petrified.

She had no reason to be. She knew she was being illogical, but she had this unrelenting fear that something would go wrong with her pregnancy. If it did, she told herself as she entered the clinic with clammy hands and an upset stomach, it was better that Jasper wasn't here to watch her fall apart.

It would mean, however, that she and Jasper had lost their linchpin. Without this baby holding them together, what else would they have? That was what she was really afraid of.

They had grown a little closer over the last weeks as they began to intertwine their lives more fully. Dare she say, they were becoming friends? They flirted and made bad jokes and, if they happened to disagree on something, managed to work through it without tearing the other down.

It wasn't strong enough to withstand a loss, though.

"Vienna? *Hola*, Mami." The technician was very warm and chatty as she confirmed Vienna's information and asked her how many weeks along she was.

"Twelve yesterday." If she counted the two weeks before she and Jasper had even met, which the doctors seemed to think was important.

"You're nervous?" the woman asked with a shrewd look at Vienna's apprehensive face. "It can be uncomfortable, but it won't hurt."

"I've been waiting to tell people until I know this scan shows everything is well," she admitted, watching closely as the woman smeared cold jelly on her abdomen. She searched the woman's cheerful expression for clues, as if the technician had X-ray vision and could tell anything just from looking at her.

The instrument was about to touch her skin when there was a knock on the door.

"I'm sorry to interrupt." A woman cracked the door, poking her head in. "Mr. Lindor is here. May he join you?"

"What?" Vienna lifted her head. "Yes," she hurried to say.

"Is that Papi?" the technician asked. "Come, come. You can stand over there."

Jasper looked every bit as powerfully handsome as he had this morning when he'd shrugged on that light gray suit jacket and kissed her goodbye. The pale glow from the ultrasound screen made his expression difficult to read, but the kiss on her brow was tender enough to leaving a lingering tingle.

"I thought you were busy?" She was floored that he had made this a priority.

"I told them to fly to site without me. If I can't trust my team, why did I hire them?" He picked up her hand and squeezed gently. "Is everything okay?"

"We're just starting." The technician pressed a dull, hard instrument against Vienna's abdomen.

Vienna gritted her teeth against the discomfort of her full bladder, waiting for—

"Here's your baby's heart." The woman pointed to a fluttering glow on the screen.

"Oh," Vienna sighed with relief. Tears came into her eyes.

Jasper wove his fingers with hers. In a very visceral way, she felt each of those flutters traveling through both of them, fusing them together.

"And already posing for selfies," the technician teased, clicking when the baby's profile came into focus. "You can use that for your announcement," she told Vienna.

"We can tell people?" Jasper asked, voice not quite steady. He looked to Vienna. "No more worries?"

Logically, she knew the twelve-week mark was not a clear line that guaranteed anything. It only meant it was less likely that loss could happen, but emotionally it was a tremendous milestone for her. It was one that choked her up with joy at the miracle she was finally letting herself believe could come true.

"Vi," Jasper asked in a hushed voice, caressing her wet cheek. "What's wrong?"

"Nothing. Nothing is wrong and that makes me really, really happy."

"Me, too." He pressed his smile to hers.

Jasper had rushed back to his office for the afternoon, but he came home early, surprising Vienna where she was cooling off in the pool, still metaphorically floating after seeing the evidence of their growing baby. It was real!

"Oh. Hello," she said when he appeared in his swimsuit. It was a low-waist, snug black band that underlined his six-pack abs and stretched across his flat hips, barely containing his gear. He didn't say anything, only dove straight in, not surfacing until he was beside her in the shallow end where she sat on the stairs.

"Honey, I'm home," he said when he popped up. He kissed her, beard and lips wet as he lingered with his greeting. When he drew back, she was as breathless as if she had swum the length of the pool underwater.

"So you are." She was insubstantial as he gathered her in his arms and stole her seat on the stairs, guiding her into his lap. "How was the rest of your day?" she asked.

"Good. We passed muster and can move to next steps."

"That's good news!"

"It is."

"Not least of which is that we get to continue spending winters here, where it's summer. I'm officially a snowbird," she said, referring to the Canadians who flew south in October. "Why do they even call them that when they're trying to escape the snow?"

"Right? Team sunfish. The more time I get to see you in a bikini, the better."

"This is probably my last day in a bikini for a while," she said ruefully, patting the distinct roundness that was starting to show in her middle.

"Don't get self-conscious on my account." His hand was on her hip and his thumb stroked toward her navel. "I think you're cute as hell." He shifted her so her bottom was more firmly in the cradle of his thighs. "Did you talk to anyone at home?"

"I wanted to wait for you." She played her fingers over his ear and the back of his neck. "I kind of want to do it in person, but also, I can't wait until spring. What do you think of going home for Christmas?"

"Amelia asked me the other day what our plans were. I said I'd check with you. I think we should go home. When we do, we could…" He tipped her slightly and his hand worked under her thigh.

"You're usually better at this," she said blithely, while hanging on around his neck so she didn't fall into the water.

"I have something in my trunks."

"I'm familiar with the contents of your trunks. I'm pretty sure you're off the mark there, too."

"You think you're so funny." Amusement was glinting in his eyes. "There's a pocket in them."

"Where? And for *what*? If you have your phone in there, I will be very impressed." She wiggled, trying to see, but whatever he wanted was in his fist.

"When we go home, let's make this official." He opened his hand to show her a ring with a vivid blue stone that flashed purple in the light. The platinum setting was elegant in its simplicity.

"Jasper! That's beautiful. Sapphire?"

"Blue diamond. They're very rare. This one is ethically sourced. I checked. I thought it suited a woman who is the diamond of diamonds."

"Flatterer," she accused, but she was genuinely moved by his words. "You've already given me the most precious thing I could ever want, though." She meant their baby.

"I'm being sincere." He cupped her cheek, waiting for her eyes to meet his. "You are very special, Vienna Waverly. Remarkable. Not just for this beautiful miracle you're creating, but for the very specific sparkle you bring to my life. I'm in awe of you every day—as an artist and as a woman who is starting a new life on her own terms. I already know you'll be an amazing mother to our child. Will you marry me?"

How could she say no? It wasn't a declaration of love, but he was making a point of telling her this wasn't just about their baby. For the first time in her life, she felt as though someone really saw her and valued her and *wanted* her. That meant everything.

Her throat closed up with emotion so she

could only whisper, "Yes." She held out her hand for him to thread the ring onto her finger.

As he did, an old wives' tale came to her, something her grandmother had told her as a child. She had said the wedding ring went on the left ring finger because there was a direct vein from that finger up her arm and into her heart.

It certainly felt that way as Jasper slid the ring into place. A sweet sensation arrowed into her chest and, even though she had never felt anything like it, she knew what it was: love. True love. The kind she had always wished for.

The words hovered in a glow around her heart, glittering and fragile in their newness.

His mouth covered hers before she could say them aloud, which was okay. She wasn't ready yet and, pretty soon, she forgot about anything except where her bikini had gone and what else he had in his trunks.

CHAPTER TWELVE

VIENNA USED HER connections at home—Jasper was still trying to get her friends straight, but he was pretty sure she called the one Hunter had jilted—to squeeze the only available date out of a boutique hotel in Toronto. It had been converted from a nineteenth-century bank and they were booked solid for the busy holiday season, but they'd had a last-minute midweek cancellation.

They sent out invites, but kept the baby news to themselves. After a busy month of making arrangements from afar, they landed mere days before their nuptials, into a typical snowy, blustery Ontario storm.

Jasper didn't mind the weather. It gave them an excuse to stay in while Vienna slept off her jet lag. He did relent and allow his sister and her family to invade the first afternoon they were back. Truthfully, he was excited to see Amelia's reaction to the baby news and she did not disappoint. She screamed.

Peyton was so startled that she cried and needed a cuddle with Mommy to calm down, but the adults were laughing and Amelia said, "I'm going to cry for days. I'm so happy for you both. For all of us." She kept hugging each of them, even Hunter and Peyton, unable to contain her elation.

"Vi." Hunter was quieter in his reaction.

Jasper tensed, not caring what Hunter might say to him, but he was damned protective of Vienna's feelings. If her brother was the least bit offside, they would have a very serious conversation.

But Hunter's eyes were damp when he said, "This is really great news. Congratulations. Both of you." He shook Jasper's hand with genuine warmth.

Jasper tried not to let the sentiment get to him, but the way Vienna looked so incandescent humbled him. It was a moment of pure shared happiness. Moments like this were as rare as that blue diamond she wore and as close to perfection as anything could get.

Guilt speared into him even as he basked in it, smearing a streak of darkness across the day. If only Orlin Caulfield wasn't also enjoying life to the fullest. The last report had placed him somewhere in the South Pacific, still evading any sort of law enforcement or consequences for his actions.

"What's wrong?" Vienna asked, touching his arm. She was always tuned in to his moods.

"Nothing." Jasper shook off his grim thoughts. He wouldn't ruin this for her. Or Amelia.

But even as he held his niece and imagined holding his own baby soon, all he could think about was Saqui, and the fact he would never get to experience this at all.

Jasper seemed remote over the next few days. Vienna put it down to how busy they were.

They drove to see his father, so they could share the baby news in person. Tobias was delighted and promised to see them again soon. He was bringing a date, Ola, to their wedding, but they wouldn't arrive until the morning of the ceremony.

Once all the family had been informed, they made a public announcement confirming that Vienna Waverly was newly engaged, and yes, she was pregnant, and yes, she was marrying Jasper Lindor at a downtown hotel a week before Christmas.

Paparazzi were soon braving the sleeting

weather and thick holiday traffic to photograph them as they left her apartment to run a few errands.

"That's another thing I love about Santiago," Vienna mused in the car. "No one cares who I am there."

It wasn't the most profound statement, but Jasper didn't respond, seeming distracted.

"Is everything all right?" she asked. "I'm sorry about the party tonight, but people expect to see me there."

"My sister expects me to be there," he pointed out dryly.

"True." It was more of an obligation to Hunter, though. Her brother had always been efficient with his socializing. He hosted two or three huge parties throughout the year, inviting all the celebrities and business contacts who expected it. Vienna had often played hostess in the past, so she knew practically everyone who was invited. "I could be indisposed if you prefer to stay home."

"I don't mind. I still feel like the blue-collar boy from Goderich, but you always make these things very easy to bear."

"That's funny. You're the one who makes it easy for me." They had hosted several of their own parties full of high-profile strangers in

Santiago. Vienna still suffered a certain tension, expecting a drunken spectacle like her stepmother used to provide, but Jasper made a good wingman. He knew how to talk *fútbol* and business opportunities while she leaned into arts and culture.

They were turning into quite the power couple, she thought with amusement as they parted. She had a fitting for her wedding gown, but was also picking up the dress she would wear to tonight's party.

Jasper was out when she returned, which made her wonder where he'd gone, but he was home by the time she rose from a brief nap. The party was black tie, so he dressed in a tuxedo, one tailored to accentuate his shoulders and wedged frame. His beard had been trimmed and his hair was professionally tousled.

"You look amazing."

"So do you." His gaze nearly incinerated the blue sequined gown right off her body. His attention flowed down her abundant cleavage to where her little bump was proudly front and center. "You don't need any adornments, but when you said you were wearing blue, I thought these would go with your dress. Maybe not." He showed her a pair of earrings. "Tourmalines. They're from Brazil."

They were a startling neon blue with icy diamonds surrounding them.

"I love them!" she gasped. "I'm definitely wearing them." She removed the simple diamond studs she had put in her lobes. "We'll call it an early Christmas present."

"Actually, I have something else for under the tree." He scratched beneath his beard.

"Wedding gift?"

"Same."

"Jasper. Do you buy these for me? Or for yourself?" she asked with teasing suspicion. He had told her once that he was single because he had a small obsession with rocks. He seemed to take a lot of pleasure in finding rare and beautiful gemstones for her, not that she minded in the least.

"Little of both," he admitted ruefully. "I get to look at them when you wear them, so that's definitely a win for me. Did you know there's something called a push present?"

"You're incorrigible," she chuckled.

For a moment, he seemed to have shed whatever heavy mood he'd been wearing. They were smiling and lost in each other's eyes and the words were right there. *I love you.*

The doorman buzzed.

"That will be the car," he said and crooked

his arm in invitation. "Come on. I want to show you off."

"Me, or these earrings?"

"You," he insisted, lifting her spirits even more.

The party was a crush, filled with pro-athletes, Canadian film and music stars, and executives from various corporations.

For the first time in memory, Vienna was completely relaxed as she circulated with Jasper. She felt as though she had rewritten her life with a far better ending. She was in love with her fiancé, expecting his baby. In two days they would marry. Everything was finally going right for her.

As the party reached its height, Hunter gave a toast. First, he thanked his guests for coming, and thanked Amelia for putting together such a wonderful bash. They shared a look of naked adoration that had Vienna swallowing a lump of emotion.

"Finally, I'd like to offer a toast to my brother-in-law, Jasper, who is soon to be my brother-in-law." Hunter cleared his throat and waited for the chuckles to subside. "And my sister, Vienna, who kept me sane through some very rough years. I'm so proud of you for going after the love and happiness you so rightly deserve. To Jasper and Vienna."

Vienna felt Jasper's arm come around her as he raised his champagne and she lifted her sparkling cranberry juice. His lips touched her temple and she made herself smile, but Hunter's words were echoing in her ears like a death knell.

The love and happiness you so rightly deserve...

Did she have that, though?

Vienna was still trying to shake off her doubts the next afternoon. She and Jasper had a great relationship, one that built her confidence and gave her the other things she had so wanted in her life—art, a baby.

But the other vital thing she had wanted was love.

Jasper went out for the morning, joining college friends for coffee since they couldn't make the wedding, but he wanted to see them while he was in town.

Vienna had needed a quiet morning anyway. She woke feeling headachy and vaguely nauseous, which she put down to the late night at Hunter's party and grazing all that rich and sugary food. Maybe she had picked up a bug from travel. Her cheeks felt hot while the rest of her was chilled, but she told herself her pregnant body was having trouble adjusting to the switch from summer warmth to subzero winter and relentless central heat. A quick text to her maternity nurse, who had returned to Vancouver for the holidays, told Vienna she could have an over-the-counter headache tablet if she wanted one.

Vienna took one and it seemed to help. She felt less touchy when Jasper returned and they left for the hotel. They were having their final meeting with the wedding planner and touring the rooms where the wedding ceremony and reception would be held. Soon, the wedding party would arrive for the rehearsal, then they would all have dinner.

Due to the short notice, their guest list was only three hundred, but they had spared no expense, starting with booking this venue. It was stunning. The Renaissance architecture featured arched windows and high, ornate ceilings, imposing columns, and polished brass rails. They would marry in a gallery where a bower had been set up against heavy wooden doors. After the vows, while they were having their photos taken in the vault turned wine cellar, the guests would enter the main hall where they would be entertained by bartenders who spun and juggled bottles while serving cocktails at the long bar.

The reception ballroom was decorated in a winter theme with frosted red roses in tall crystal vases standing like icicles in circles of holly. Tartan throw blankets were draped over the backs of chairs as gifts for the guests. Handwritten calligraphy place cards were propped up in pine cones, and sparkling snowflakes hung from the ceiling. Candles in lanterns were waiting to be lit.

"I'll leave you to enjoy this while I check on the gift bags. I know everything arrived, but staff may still be assembling them. This is genius, by the way. I will be stealing this idea for future guests." The specialist touched a button on her way out the door, lowering the lights.

A projection of the night sky appeared on the ceiling with the aurora borealis flickering in streaks of green and purple dancing across it.

"Wow." Jasper tilted back his head so Vienna couldn't see his expression, but he sounded awed. "You made all of this happen in a few weeks?"

"I wanted it to be perfect."

"It is. You are." He reached for her.

She nudged up against him, both of them watching the ceiling a moment longer.

"Jasper." She had to know.

"Yes?" He looked down on her with tenderness and cupped her cheek. "Oh. You're nice and warm."

"I love you," she said, heart in her throat as she searched his eyes.

She saw the shift in his gaze to caution and it stole the floor right out from under her. She was falling into an abyss all by herself.

Oh, God.

"You don't love me," she realized in horror while old voices asked, *Why would he*?

"Vi. I care about you very much. You know that." His hands firmed on her, as if he sensed her slipping away and was trying to hold on to her.

She pressed until he released her, all of her going hot and cold as her profound mistake crashed over her in churning waves.

"I'm doing it again," she realized with horror. A terrible burn seared up from the pit of her belly into the back of her throat. "I'm getting caught up in creating the appearance of perfection, but that's not what this is."

"There is no such thing as perfection. You

know that." His tone hardened. "What we have is very, very good, though."

"I thought we were falling in love, Jasper! I thought if I gave you time…" How long had she waited last time? *Years.* She felt so stupid. *Again.* "*Can* you love me? *Will* you?" Oh, she felt pathetic asking that, but she had to know. Had to.

"I can't see into the future, Vi. What I can promise is to always be honest with you."

She recoiled from that.

"But you haven't *been* honest. You've made me think…" Had he, though? Or was she the one who had interpreted every gesture as burgeoning love? She had seen what she wanted to see, mistaking kindness and decency for something more than that. That was how little she'd had of those things!

The stupid lights were making her sick, so she impatiently moved to the door.

"Vienna!" he shouted behind her.

She smacked the switches to put on the main lights, washing out the romantic sky with cold, clinical white.

For a moment they stared at each other across the sea of colorless crystal and faux snow and unlit candles.

Jasper's jaw was clenched tight, his chest rising in agitated breaths. "You're acting as if a couple of words would change what we have."

"They do!" she cried. "I just said them and you didn't. That changes *everything*."

"It does not," he asserted firmly. "We're still getting married, we're still having a baby, we're still building a life together."

"On what?" She flung up helpless hands. "On me feeling *again* like I'm giving everything while my husband offers me nothing?"

"It's hardly nothing, Vi," he shot back darkly.

"Of *yourself*. You are asking me to wake up every morning knowing I'm in love with you while you don't love me. That's even worse than neither of us feeling any love! I can't do it. I won't."

What was she saying? She covered her mouth, already seeing the canceled wedding and another huge scandal.

She grasped onto the wall, so nauseated she was dizzy with it.

"Vienna," he growled. "Don't make threats you're not prepared to back up."

"Do you really want to marry someone you don't love?" she asked him with anguish. "Take it from me, Jasper, it's not great." She was shaking, her whole body chilled, but sweaty. "I think I'm going to throw up."

"This is cold feet. Let's sit down—" He yanked out a chair. "Let's talk this out."

"No. I'm literally…" Her stomach was curdling. The chill on her skin deepened. She hurried away, rushing to where she'd seen the door to the ladies' room earlier.

Jasper started after her, but decided they could use a minute to cool off.

He looked around and saw…

He swore and rubbed his eyes.

He saw how much care she'd put into this wedding. How much it meant to her. He saw love.

He also saw a culmination of everything he'd been seeing and hearing since their return to Canada. Just this morning, he'd heard it again from one of his old college buddies.

"You've really got it all, eh? You're living the dream."

He was. He was at the top of his professional game, had a beautiful fiancée, a wedding planned and a baby on the way. What more did anyone need?

Love. Of course Vi wanted love.

He could barely accept it from her, though, let alone offer it. Which would crush her if he dared to say it, but all of this was so much more than he deserved. Not when—

"What kind of wife do you want?" Saqui had asked him one day while they were hiking into a valley.

"Are you placing an order?" Jasper asked dryly.

"Online," Saqui said with a swish of his finger to indicate swiping. "But they keep sending the wrong one." He grinned his mischievous grin.

"Yeah?" Jasper chuckled, expecting Saqui was working up to a tall tale on his dating antics. "What are you looking for, then?"

Saqui took him seriously, pressing his bottom lip with thought.

"Someone who thinks about things. Pretty would be nice, but she has to be kind. And she has to like dogs. I want her to make me laugh. She had better cook," he decided with a grimace.

That made Jasper chuckle again because they had established that Saqui was a terrible cook.

"Why are you so eager to marry?" Jasper had to ask. "Are you saving yourself for your wife?"

"No," Saqui chuckled. "But I want to hurry up and meet her. This…" He scanned the hillside they were scaling. "What we're doing is interesting, but it doesn't mean anything. This isn't my life. *She* will be."

Whenever Jasper thought about that conversation, he thought about the poor girl out there somewhere who would never get to meet the man who had been so anxious to find her.

"Where's Vienna?" Amelia asked, yanking Jasper out of his agonizing memories.

Amelia and Hunter were Vienna's matron of honor and escort down the aisle. Jasper's father, Tobias, would stand up for him as best man and two of Jasper's cousins were coming in with his father in the morning to be groomsmen.

Would the wedding even go ahead? Jasper's heart lurched.

"She went to the ladies' room. Would you check on her for me?" He was starting to suspect she'd left altogether.

He pinched the bridge of his nose, unable to look at Hunter when Hunter asked gravely, "Is everything all right?"

"We had an argument," Jasper admitted.

"About?"

Cold feet, he wanted to say, but that wasn't true at all.

He didn't get a chance to reply. Someone else arrived.

"Hunter."

"Remy." Hunter shook the man's hand with the familiarity of long friendship. There was ruefulness in his tone when he greeted Remy's partner, briefly kissing her cheek. "Eden. Good to see you. You look wonderful. Congratulations." He nodded at the baby bump she revealed as she unbuttoned her coat.

Vienna had worriedly asked Amelia how she felt about her inviting Eden, the bride Hunter had thrown over for Amelia, to be her bridesmaid along with someone named Quinn. Amelia had said it was time she properly met everyone.

"It's good to see you, too," Eden said to Hunter, seeming sincere if sheepish and amused by her equal rush to the altar with someone else.

"Quinn, Micah. Have you all met Vienna's groom?" Hunter introduced the second pair as they came in.

Jasper wanted nothing less in the world than to meet new people right now. He gave everyone distracted handshakes, looking past them for his bride.

This isn't my life. She *will be.*

Something hard was lodged in his throat, making it hard to breathe.

"Where are Vi and Amelia?" Remy looked around.

"I'm wondering that myself," Jasper said tightly and started for the door.

At that moment, Amelia rushed back in. She was pale, eyes wide with alarm.

"I've called an ambulance. Jasper…" The look on her face sent a sword straight through his heart. "Vienna is having stomach pains. She can't walk."

"Vi." Jasper burst into the ladies' room and dropped to the floor in front of where Vienna had curled up on an upholstered bench.

"She has a fever," the hotel's first aid attendant was saying as he read the instrument he had just aimed at her forehead. He relayed the number into the phone.

Jasper cupped her cheek and tried to dry the tear tracking from her eye onto her nose.

She couldn't take the look of anguish on his face and closed her eyes against it.

"No bleeding. How many weeks?" the attendant asked.

"Seventeen and a half," Jasper said. "Can you check the heartbeat?"

"Not with a stethoscope. Too early in the

pregnancy." The attendant offered a tight look of apology.

Jasper tried to take her hand, but she drew it away, wanting to keep it on the side of her bump. She was certain she had felt a flutter there. Did she, though? Or was that more wishful thinking?

The stabbing pain was relentless, sitting there angry and horrific, making her sick. She just wanted to be left alone with her agony, but people kept asking her stupid questions about when it had started and what she had eaten and what sorts of medications she was on.

Now the first responders were here, making her shift onto the bed, touching her and—

"Let me do it," Jasper snarled, then ever so gently stroked her hair. "Okay, Vi? Can you hold on to my neck? I'm going to move you onto the stretcher."

He gathered her as carefully as he could, but she was still biting her lips as he moved her, moaning with protest. It hurt *so much*.

They covered her with a blanket and hurried to roll the stretcher outside where snowflakes melted against her hot face. Jasper climbed into the ambulance with her, taking her hand in two of his while the attendant poked something into the back of her other hand and asked her to help him time how quickly the pains were coming.

"It's one long pain," she said for the thousandth time, clenching her wet eyes. "Even my own baby doesn't want me."

"Vi." Jasper had never felt so helpless in his life. He would do anything, *anything*, to stop this from happening. He was agonized at the thought of losing their baby. It would kill him, but he *could not bear* what it would do to Vienna.

How could he have been so stupid earlier, when he had felt guilty for "having it all." He should have been on his knees with gratitude. He *knew* how fragile life was, but he had still taken his good fortune for granted. This incredible woman had told him she loved him and he hadn't wanted to hear it because it was more good on top of good. Too much good. He hadn't felt entitled to that much happiness.

He had met the woman who would be his life, but he hadn't wanted to fully embrace her and all that he felt for her because of guilt. Guilt that he held up like a shield so he wouldn't have to suffer the grief that waited behind it.

"Vienna, listen to me." He had to consciously keep himself from crushing her hand. "I love you. Do you hear me? No matter what happens, I love you and I want you to marry me. *You*."

"You don't have to say that." Her lips quivered.

"I do have to say it," he said grimly. "I should have said it an hour ago, but—" He swore under his breath. "An hour ago, I was afraid to let myself need you, as if it hadn't already happened. How would I cope if I lost you?" He pressed the back of her hand to his cheek, only becoming aware tears were leaking from his eyes when she caught her breath and shifted her finger against his wet skin.

"I didn't know fear an hour ago. Not this kind. Now I do. I love you. You are everything to me. Whatever happens, you are not alone right now. I'm right here beside you and I will stay beside you. Okay?"

She blinked her matted lashes, choking, "It's just s-so unfair."

"It is." He leaned over her and stroked her brow. "But let's be thankful this baby came into our lives and brought us together. Right now, we're still all three together, hmm?"

She nodded and clung to his hand, not saying anything more until they arrived at the hospital where she was wheeled into the emergency room and quickly assessed.

"The fetal heart rate is elevated," the doctor said as the instruments were hooked up.

They both looked to each other with tentative hope.

"There's a heartbeat," Jasper confirmed, squeezing that news into Vienna's arm.

She nodded through her tears of distress while the doctor ordered an ultrasound and promised to give her something for the pain.

A few minutes later, she was wheeled into a similar imaging room to the one that had made them so happy in Santiago. This time, the technician was somber, but she quicky identified the baby's heartbeat. The baby was moving, too.

"Are you having contractions?" the technician asked.

"I don't know what this pain is. It's constant."

The technician continued to torture her, pressing into a spot that made Vienna nearly scream. She stuck her fingernails into the back of Jasper's hand.

"Be careful," Jasper growled at the woman.

The technician nodded with concern and the doctor was brought in.

"You're not miscarrying," the doctor said after consulting the screen. "You have appendicitis. You need surgery. Tonight."

Jasper's heart fell as quickly as it had lifted.

"But—what about the baby?" Vienna asked, mouth trembling.

"We do it laparoscopically. The risk to your pregnancy is low. We'll begin prepping you immediately."

She looked to Jasper, openly afraid.

He swallowed down his helplessness. He couldn't bear it. He cupped the side of her face, looking deeply into her eyes.

"I love you. Whatever happens, *I love you.* I'm not going anywhere," he swore.

Jasper was allowed to stay with her until they took her to the OR. When he walked into the waiting room, Amelia and Hunter were there, both pale with concern.

"Appendicitis," Jasper said, running his hand through his hair. "It doesn't seem to have burst, so that's a silver lining. They said surgery will take an hour."

"Surgery," Hunter repeated in a hollow voice. His gaze went to the doors where Jasper had come through. He looked as though he wanted to go find his sister and see for himself.

"What about the baby?" Amelia asked anxiously.

"Okay for now." Jasper sat down, knees no

longer able to hold him, quietly begging his friend to do what he could to give him a second chance.

I'll get it right this time, Saqui. I promise.

Amelia moved to sit beside him and wordlessly hugged his arm, leaving her head tilted against her shoulder. Then she reached out her hand to Hunter, beckoning him to sit on her other side so she could hold his hand, too.

How could Vienna have ever worried her brother would disown her? Hunter was as wrecked by this as Jasper was. If Amelia wasn't between them, they would be clinging to each other.

Hunter shifted once, taking out his phone and replying to a text, murmuring, "Remy," but otherwise they sat like that the whole time, wordless, holding on to each other while they waited for news.

Finally, a nurse came in to say, "She's in recovery. Everything went well. The baby's vitals are strong, too. You can see her shortly," she said to Jasper. "Only one visitor, I'm afraid."

"I'll call Dad," Amelia said with a shaken sigh. She rose when Jasper did and hugged him. "It's going to be okay now."

He sure as hell hoped so.

Amelia placed the call and moved into a

corner while Hunter pushed his hands into his pockets and studied him. Jasper realized he had never told him what his argument with Vienna was about.

"I'll call off the wedding," Hunter said.

"No," Jasper asserted. "I said some stupid things to her, but I love her and told her so. She loves me, too. No one is ever going to work harder than I will at making her happy. We're getting married."

"I'm pleased to hear it," Hunter said with a trace of amusement coming in at the edges of his somber expression. "Vienna made choices years ago that I had to respect, but I knew she was shortchanging herself. I've always hated myself for not trying harder to dissuade her. I need to know she's marrying someone who sees how incredible she is. I *want* you to marry her. God knows, that will make my wife happy and that's all *I* want. But I don't think Vienna is going to make it to the ceremony tomorrow."

Jasper swore and shut his eyes.

"I meant that I'll deal with informing the hotel and the guests." Hunter was definitely laughing at him. "Based on experience, I suggest letting the guests eat the food and drink you've paid for. It goes a long way toward smoothing everything over."

"Thanks. Have a great time," Jasper said wryly. "Take photos so we know what we missed."

Jasper wouldn't miss anything except the vows. He needed that formal connection to her more than ever now.

The nurse came to get him as Amelia finished her call to their father. "Dad will still come tomorrow. He wants to see all of us and make sure Vienna is okay."

Jasper nodded.

"Do you want us to wait and take you back to the hotel?" Hunter offered.

"No, I'll stay with her as long as they'll let me."

"Give her our love," Hunter said.

"I will." Jasper hurried to Vienna's side.

Every time Vienna woke over the next two days, Jasper was there. Each time, he reassured her that the baby was doing well, that she was recovering nicely, and that he loved her.

"The wedding," she said plaintively when she got enough of her faculties back to remember it.

"The cocktail show was a big hit, as was the improvised snowball fight," he said dryly.

"Oh? Did Amelia go? I love Eden and Quinn, but I was so worried she would feel awkward with them."

"She said she spent a lot of the night chatting with them. She thinks they're great."

"Oh, that makes me happy. Did you go?"

His frown scolded her for even suggesting it. "When I go to *our* wedding, you'll be there." He brought her palm to his lips, pressing a kiss there. "You will marry me, won't you?"

A latent misgiving struck. "Maybe I was putting too much pressure on our relationship." She could see now that the pageantry of the wedding had been one of her old coping strategies, where she had projected the grand romance she had longed for.

"That's not true at all." He hitched his hip on the bed and pressed her hand to his thigh. "I couldn't take being this happy, Vi. It was hard to accept your love when Saqui will never have what we have, but he would be the first to say, *Love her, you fool*. He knew how rare and special it is to find the person you want to spend your life with. He would be angry with me for wasting a single minute of our time. So would my father, for that matter. Love is scary. Loss hurts."

His mouth flattened and he continued to iron her hand to his thigh.

"I was using my guilt and anger over Saqui's death to buffer my grief, so I didn't have to face it and feel it. Rather than dealing with the pain, I put it between us. On you. I won't do that again. I promise."

"You miss him a lot." She turned her hand so she was holding his.

"I do." His brow flexed. "But I have to accept that he's gone. Putting Orlin Caulfield in jail won't bring Saqui back, so I won't obsess over that anymore. It's important to me that he be caught and brought to trial, but I'll let the authorities handle it. That isn't my life. You are. Both of you." He released her hand to set his palm on the top of her bump. "I'm so glad you and the baby are going to be all right. I don't know what I would have done without you, I really don't."

She covered his knuckles, so moved by his naked honesty she could hardly speak.

"I let my own ghosts come between us when I said you don't give me anything." She felt so remorseful for saying that. "You give me everything. My life with you is the one I always wanted. I would be honored to marry you, Jasper."

They married a few days after she was discharged, on the morning of Christmas Eve. Vienna was still moving slowly, but feeling much better. She put on her wedding dress, which was a classic ivory silk with a crossover top and a satin sash. Since she thought they were simply meeting the wedding officiant at the hotel for a private ceremony, she didn't bother with the tiara and veil or even a bouquet.

She was greeted with a miniature version of their wedding decor in an intimate lounge. The arbor was in place before a marble fireplace where a fire crackled merrily.

Vienna gasped as she took that in along with the dozen smiling faces.

"My cousins are home with their families, but these guys were happy to step in."

He meant Eden and Remy, and Quinn and Micah, who were standing with Tobias and Ola. Hunter held Peyton, who was in layers of silk and tule. Amelia was trying to put a band of silk flowers on her head, but Peyton pulled it right off.

The baby smiled when she saw Vienna. Everyone did.

"I can't believe this!" she said to Jasper, touched to the bottoms of her feet.

"We wanted to come," Eden said.

"Yeah. You scared us the other day," Remy said, coming forward to give her a gentle hug.

"You came all the way to Germany for our wedding," Quinn said.

"We weren't going to miss yours," Micah agreed.

"Shall we get started?" the officiant said in a gentle nudge.

The women arranged themselves to the left of the arbor, the men on the right. Ola took Peyton to lead Vienna and Hunter down the short stretch of carpet that formed the aisle.

"He really loves you, you know. We all do. *I* do," Hunter said in a quiet, sincere undertone as he offered his arm to her.

"I know." She hugged his arm. "But thank you. I like hearing it. I love you, too."

They started to walk. Her pulse tripped with enchantment, taking in everything from the soft notes of an unseen harp to the light shining from her groom's eyes.

Jasper was profoundly handsome in his morning suit. He took both her hands as she joined him. His eyes were damp with joyous emotion. So were hers.

They spoke their simple vows in strong, confident voices and, when they kissed, they were both smiling. The spark of passion was always there, though, keeping her lips clinging to his as he tenderly brushed at the happy tear on her cheek.

"I never imagined I could feel this way about

anyone," he told her, right there in front of all their witnesses. "I love you with everything in me."

She hadn't known she could feel this much love, either. Or that she could let it spring out of her, confident that Jasper would catch it and hold it with such tender care.

"I love you, too." She had never felt so truly loved, so surrounded by love, in her life.

EPILOGUE

Almost one year later

"I PROMISE YOU, son, that if you let yourself sleep, the whole world becomes a brighter place," Jasper told Finley Tobias Saqui Lindor.

The infant interrupted his own overtired cry to give a big yawn that showed his four tiny front teeth. He scrubbed his fist into his eye and started to cry again.

His first nap of the day had been interrupted by workmen downstairs, but he was a little too much like his father, pushing himself when he wanted something. Today, he wanted to not relax and nod off.

He wasn't hungry, having almost fallen asleep while Vienna had fed him a few minutes ago. Jasper had then brought him up here, thinking he would fall right asleep, but no. He had decided to get some things off his chest first.

Jasper didn't mind an excuse to pace the room that was decorated with yellow ducks between the green stripes in the wallpaper, rubbing the back of his grouchy son. He knew what a privilege this was.

"I thought we had a gentlemen's agreement about this, though," he chided softly. "We're both working on better sleep habits. I will if you will."

Jasper's insomnia meant that he'd been hands-on from the earliest days—and nights—with their newborn. They were both getting better at sleeping longer stretches, though. The turning point for Jasper had been when Orlin Caulfield had stopped at Rapa Nui for provisions. He'd been apprehended and was now in the custody of Chilean authorities.

"What's holding you back? Hmm?" Jasper asked his son. "Are you angry Mommy's working so much? She's getting ready for her show. If you knew how many of her sketches were of you, you might not be so put out."

Fin finally took the pacifier and quieted. His eyes drifted closed and his small body relaxed into sleep.

Jasper very carefully eased him into his crib, taking an extra minute to absorb those miniature echoes of his wife in Fin's features. The peak in his barely-there brow and the shape of his ear and the color of his fine hair.

As he turned to the door, he found Vienna waiting there, watching them, her face wearing the serene love that filled him with such humble gratitude.

He touched his lips and joined her outside the room, bringing the baby monitor and gently closing the door behind himself.

"You didn't have to come up. He's asleep."

"The workmen left, so hopefully he'll get a full nap this time," she said, smiling at the screen.

Fin was a ball of energy who kept them firmly on their toes, then this—a cherub who mesmerized until he woke and burst into chortles and bounces and squirms all over again. He had already started to crawl, much to their terrified delight. His near daily swim was his absolute favorite time of day, so a plexiglass fence was being installed around the pool tomorrow, long before they really needed it, but Peyton would be here soon and she *ran*.

Hunter and Amelia were bringing Tobias and Ola for Christmas. They were arriving Friday and staying through the holidays. Then, since Micah and Quinn were joining Remy and Eden in the Caribbean, the foursome had proposed coming to Santiago to celebrate New Year's Eve with them. They were both looking forward to a fun, lively time with friends and family.

"Are you going back to work?" he asked her as she stayed here with him beside the baby's door.

"I thought we might take advantage of a quiet house before it gets very noisy and busy again." She slid her arms around his waist, pressing her curves up against him in a way that always lit his fire.

"I like how you think." He slid his hand down her hair, catching the scrunchie and releasing it from its ponytail.

"I like how you make me feel." She took his hand and led him to their bedroom.

"How's that?" His mind was already tracking down the sensual paths he planned to explore with her.

"Loved," she said simply.

His heart swelled in his chest as he pressed her to the bed beneath him. He could definitely keep doing that.

* * * * *